The Unexpected Love

The Unexpected Love

An Old Fashioned Love Story

by Rhonda Cronkhite

This book, for all intents and purposes, is a work of fiction. The love you'll read about in the story, however, is true. George and Rhonda's love story is told through the mature characters of Peter and Maggie. Most of the incidents happened exactly as told. There are a couple of times where the mature Maggie takes over. One is when Peter proposes and the other, well, I'll let you guess, but it's exactly what Rhonda would do today.

.

Table of Contents

Preface

Maggie LaHaye is a rare specimen, so they say. Whether that's good or bad, you can decide, but she's definitely figured out who she is, and who she isn't. I suppose the cuts and bruises she got while climbing up out of the ditch so many times has helped to make her who she is today. She certainly doesn't resemble the nervous young girl who felt like a soft spring rain just might do her in.

She and Sam Worthington had dated for a couple of years and enjoyed their first year of marriage when they welcomed their darling son, Luke, into their lives. It was the first of many more of these happy occasions...how many they hadn't decided and didn't really care...but it would be several. Maggie had to admit she was relieved when she learned that Sam had only been kidding when he told her he'd always wanted to call his first son Bartholomew Jonathan, just because, along with Worthington, it would have been an exceptionally long name. Sam was such a tease. Funny how things change…now it sounded like a nice tag to put on a little fellow.

Maggie says it felt like she had the world by the tail. Only five short weeks later, though, she couldn't even find the tail she'd been holding onto. Her wonderful life had come screeching to a halt, the light went out, and the sun didn't shine for a long, long time. Sam was gone and life, except for Luke, seemed meaningless.

It's almost forty years later and Maggie adamantly defends her claim that she's still never met a man who was better than Sam, and very few who were as good. In all fairness, she might be a bit biased, but at any rate, they were deeply in love.

She and Amos, her second husband, were married four and a half years later. Neither Maggie nor Amos had ever heard of bipolar disorder, but they soon discovered the havoc it can create. They had some tough times and at one point, took what they jokingly referred to as a six-year vacation.

Although she hadn't been able to live with Amos, she hoped that one day he'd get himself straightened out so they could be together again. After six years, he seemed to be doing just that and eventually moved back in with Maggie and Luke.

Living with bipolar disorder wasn't always rosy, but being a fiercely loyal woman, Maggie decided she was in this for the long haul. She would stick by Amos and help him the best that she could. That, however, is a story for another day.

The setting for this story has been changed to Vermont and New Hampshire, USA, along the Connecticut River, with the towns and villages mirroring those in real life.

Dedication

This story is dedicated to my son, George Woodworth and his sons, Jesse and Daniel. It's in honour of the man who was a part of George's and my life for all too short a time. When you arrived, George, he took on a new glow - another of his dreams had just come true and he was already making plans for all the fun you and he would have. You were definitely his pride and joy for those few short weeks.

What I lost when he died was tremendous, but what you lost can't be measured.

I've always told you what a wonderful man your dad was. My hope is that he will come alive to you through the pages of this book. Peter is truly the man your dad was, one in a million.

Jesse and Daniel, you can be proud that you're the grandsons of George Senior, even though you never got the chance to say, "Hey."

When your Aunt Esther read the story, she said it's so real that it brought George back. It's been so much fun writing and remembering. I hope you enjoy it.

It's my gift to you, my darlings.

Rhonda

Acknowledgements

One thing I learned while writing this story is that it's a whole lot more work than I realized. I also discovered that it's helpful to have a thick skin, at least in the beginning, to be able to accept the constructive criticism that has helped me to create a better story.

I'd like to thank those people whose input has made a huge difference in the finished product. I'm truly grateful for their help.

My sister-in-law, Esther Woodworth, was one of the first people to read my manuscript. She loved it, but thought I should tell it in the first person; it would be more real. That was a little hard, because, well...that meant I would be telling personal things about myself. After thinking about it, however, I had to agree with her.

Melissa Ridpath is a writer and photographer. The biggest piece of advice that Melissa gave me was even harder to accept. She wanted to know how Maggie feels when Peter looks at her that way. That's getting real personal, but I decided if anything is worth doing, it's worth doing right.

Erin Sheppard-Irwin suggested that some of Peter and Maggie's dates should be attending concerts because that's what I do in real life. And my sister really is a singer; Violet Paisley.

Leta Waugh has a degree in English and she did

the final editing of my manuscript.

Karen Dyck had endless patience with formatting the book for print, or at least I think she was patient.

Thank you all so much…no, as my dad, DeVerne Cronkhite, used to say, "Thanks ever so much!"

If you were a part of George and Rhonda's immediate circle, you may find yourself in the pages of this book. I've changed the names, however, with a couple of exceptions.

Peter's granddaughter, Marissa, is named after a little girl I fell in love with while writing the story. She just happens to be the granddaughter of one of my favourite cousins, Arnold Drost. Marissa Mills is a sweetie and when I met her, there was no other name that would do. Peter's daughter, Kendra, is named after my cousin, Kim Drost-Brooks' granddaughter, Kendra Wilson. Sam's friend, Ken, is his real name, Ken Cogswell. Peter's best friend, Judah, is the grown up Ken. All other names are randomly chosen.

The house on the back cover is the house you'll read about, along with the cement circles Maggie calls her garden art, and a birdhouse from my garden.

Maggie's Family

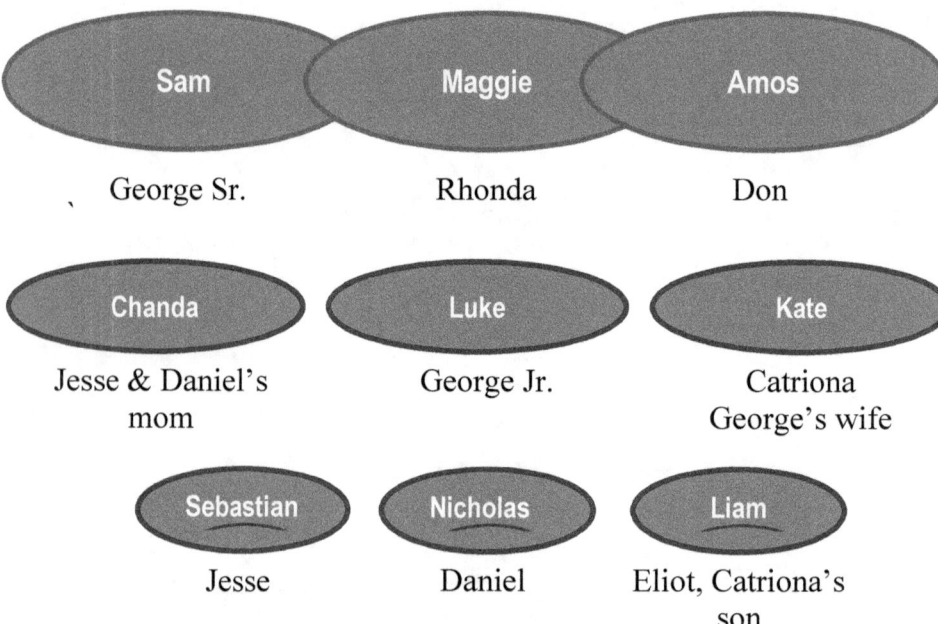

Sam
George Sr.

Maggie
Rhonda

Amos
Don

Chanda
Jesse & Daniel's mom

Luke
George Jr.

Kate
Catriona
George's wife

Sebastian
Jesse

Nicholas
Daniel

Liam
Eliot, Catriona's son

Some folks tell me they find it hard to figure out who's who. Hopefully, these simple family trees will help. Maggie's family, of course, is real, so I've indicated who they are in real life. I've given them different names in the story, just for interest sake...with the exception of Chanda.

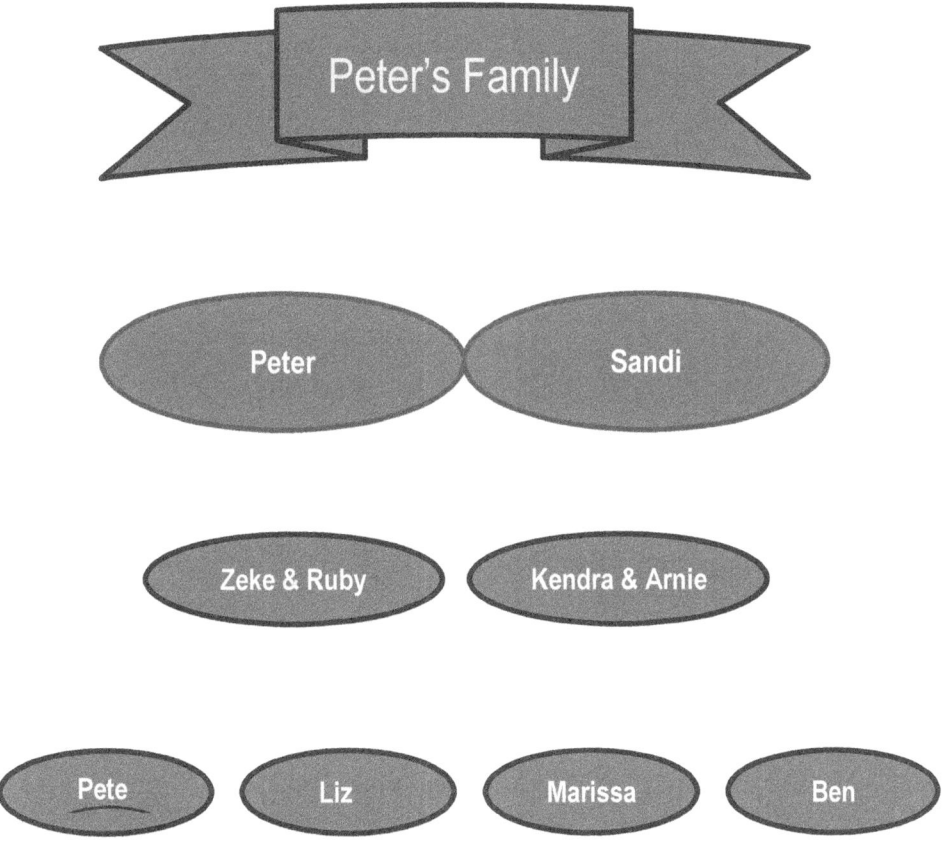

Peter's Family

Peter | Sandi

Zeke & Ruby | Kendra & Arnie

Pete | Liz | Marissa | Ben

Peter is who Rhonda believes the mature George would be today. Things that Peter likes or does, George was guilty of the same. He ate apples, core and all and he tied her curtains in knots to let the breeze blow in. He loved toasted coconut marshmallows and molasses. He usually had a lavender pomander air freshener in his truck and had coloured lights on the mirrors. When Peter tells Maggie something about his life, these are things George told Rhonda…like dishes in the sink and his views on raising children. If they could have met today, he'd most likely have been married, so these are the family members she's created.

Prologue

Picking up her journal, Maggie fingered it lovingly. Opening the cover, she traced her finger over the words, *My loving friend who holds my deepest thoughts in complete confidence.* Yes, her journal was her friend, one that had likely saved her from going completely insane, at least a time or two.

Turning the page, she read: *July 10, 2010. Thirty-seven years ago, they laid my beloved husband, his body, to rest, in the Lenentine Cemetery.*

She remembered that day all too well, a day that would be forever etched in her mind.

She'd always thought that if someone she loved died, she'd never be able to watch the coffin be put into the ground. When it happened though, she'd had three days of the worst kind of nightmare - a nightmare that had left her too numb to care. Walking away, she left the strange brown box sitting on top of the ground. She knew her beloved Sam wasn't coming back, nor was he really in that box. All that was left of him was in her heart, torn to shreds. *Let them put the box into the horrid abyss. What does it matter?*

Flipping the page, she read: *June 13, 2011. Two days ago, we laid the body of my dear husband, Amos, to rest in the Lenentine Cemetery. Amos passed away on April 5ᵗʰ. I was glad when they said the ground would be too wet to bury him right away. It would give me a little more time. Two husbands snatched away without saying 'good-bye.'*

When they finally buried Amos, she and her sister,

Rose, had even pushed the button, lowering his coffin into that dark hole. He wasn't in there either. They were both in her heart, but they were oh, so horribly elusive. She laid the book down. Sometimes it was just too much!

Remembering the pain after Sam was drowned - actual physical pain - frightened her, so she dragged her heels, dealing with it in small doses. As she sat musing one afternoon, Maggie found herself wondering what it would have been like if she and Sam had met at this stage in their lives, a more mature and settled state. After all, Maggie was twenty and Sam only twenty-one when she lost him. At fifty-eight, the only difference she could imagine was that what had been almost perfect, would be perfect. Mostly, she would share the things that the younger Maggie hadn't bothered putting into words, knowing now that tomorrow doesn't always come.

Like election day. She'd often remembered that day, smiling. Her dad was a pretty strong Democrat while Sam's family were definitely staunch Republicans. Maggie had her political opinions, but she'd never lost any sleep over who would win the next popularity contest.

When Sam had asked if she was going to vote, she'd smiled and said, "I don't think so." He'd taunted her, wanting her to vote, but ribbing her about how she'd vote.

Looking back, this was how she wished she'd done it - it was how she had really felt. "Are you sure you want me to vote, Sam?" With his teasing grin, he'd have said, "Yeah, I think you should. I'm not sure...but I think so." She'd have gone just to please him. When she returned, he'd have been grinning. "I suppose the Democrats are up one. I may as well have stayed home, eh?"

Raising her eyebrows, she'd have said, "What do you mean? There was only one name on my ticket."

At his puzzled look, she'd have said, "Why I voted for Sam Worthington. Who'd you vote for?" Sam would have been so pleased, she may have even scored an extra hug. In her mind, a husband and wife were a team, even in politics. Yes, if she were to do it over, she'd definitely know how to say those things in the moment.

It didn't take long for a story to start taking shape in her mind. After all, she knew the characters intimately and knew just how they'd act today. The more she thought about it, the more clearly she could see them...

Regardless of what has happened in my life, I still say,

"All's well that ends well."

I've read Laura Ingalls Wilder's "Little House On The Prairie" series many times. I loved it when her Pa would take everything in stride, never doling out blame, but would calmly say, *"All's well that ends well."* It's one of my mottos.

I somehow feel that my boys have taken the same outlook and I'm proud of that.

Chapter 1

A Surprise Visitor

KNEELING IN MY GARDEN BY THE SIDE STEPS, I felt the moist dirt through my glove. Looking at my hand, I saw yet another finger peeking through. I'm hard on gloves, but then I always have them on. I'd have to get another pair from the greenhouse. *Is that a car I hear?*

Gardening has been such wonderful therapy for me. I love the feel of the soil sifting through my fingers. I have a habit of pulling weeds, no matter where I am. The plants seem to be begging me to get those wretched things out of their space.

This year was different, though. I could have done with a lot less therapy. Losing Amos in April and my business in May had taken a toll on me. I had several gardens, berries needed to be transplanted, and now I'd have all the mowing to do besides. I kept busy during the days, but the evenings were long and lonely. I didn't have much company, nor did I feel like visiting after working hard all day. So I was surprised to look up and see someone coming up the drive. *No, it can't be,* I thought, but sure enough, it was. There was Peter Weatherburn in his gravel truck.

My fifty-eight-year-old heart gave a start. *I wonder what he wants? And look at me, I must be a mess.*

He stopped by the steps where I was working, looked down at me with a shy smile and said, "Hi Maggie. How are you doing?"

"Oh, I'm doing pretty well...most of the time," I answered, standing up and taking my gloves off. I absent mindedly brushed myself off and smoothed my flyaway hair. "And how about you?"

"Oh, I'm doing okay," he said. "I see you're keeping busy. You're out here working almost every time I go by. I wondered if I might be able to help with something."

Peter was charming, even with his dark blond hair rather tousled, revealing the curls that he usually kept under control. At fifty-nine, he was just starting to turn grey at the temples. He was friendly to everyone and never missed an opportunity to dish out some teasing. His easy smile was just part of his charm and his feigned ignorance to the wishful glances the females often cast in his direction was admirable.

I could hear the dogs barking inside, their faithful routine when anyone comes in the yard. "You'll have to excuse my dogs, Peter," I apologized, snapping out of my daydream. "Their manners aren't what you'd call impeccable. Yeah, I do enjoy it outside." After thinking for a moment and grateful for an excuse to grant his request, I told him I could use some topsoil.

"I have some free time this afternoon. I could get some for you."

"Oh, that would be lovely, Peter. I'll get you some money...be right back."

I hurried inside, my heart jumping around like the ladybug in a box that my grandson, Sebastian, had given me for Christmas one year. Returning with some cash, I passed it up to Peter. Flashing me a grin as he put the truck in gear, he said "At your service, ma'am," and was off.

I stood watching as he backed out the driveway. *My! That was unexpected.* I didn't know what to think...well, maybe I had an inkling, or was it just a hope? My mind wasn't going back to pulling weeds so I got a couple of shovels, let the dogs out, and wandered around checking the gardens, the dogs not far behind.

Peter was back within the hour. When he got out of his truck, he didn't seem to mind my pals all vying for his attention, while seeing who could greet him the loudest.

"Now come on, you turkeys," he said, squatting down as he affectionately patted their heads with both hands.

Cinnamon, the Maltese Poodle and my prince, was jumping up and down, while Kiwi, the charcoal Yorkie wagged her tail for dear life, her sassy bark saying, 'Don't you see me? I'm the princess!' Cookie, my Shih Tzu, patiently sat back and waited his turn. I call him the General. He doesn't mind getting his feet dirty traipsing through mud puddles, inspecting everything in his path, while Cinnamon cautiously skirts around the edges, being careful not to dirty his paws.

When the dogs finally settled down, we got to work and soon had the soil unloaded and levelled in some uneven spots on the lawn, and the rest in one of my flower beds. I looked it over, so pleased to have it done. I'd been dreading having to get several loads with my half-ton. This had been so much easier, such a blessing.

"It's beautiful out here. Would you like some lemonade? We could sit in the shade for a few minutes?" I asked, hesitantly.

"Sure. I could use a drink." As I headed inside, he headed to the garden spigot to wash his hands. *Such a gentleman!*

When I returned a few minutes later, Peter had already discovered the small sitting room I'd made under the silver maples. Holding the door open for me, he gave a little bow as I went by. I passed him the lemonade, hoping the temperature of my heart wasn't showing on my face. The dogs, ever faithful, were already waiting for me to sit down. I would end up with at least one of them on my lap, maybe two; hopefully, not all three.

"It was so nice of you to stop by and help me out, Peter," I said, sitting down and taking a few moments to get comfortable in an effort to mask the trembling hands and arms that had suddenly turned to jelly.

"I thought perhaps I could help a damsel in distress. Doesn't the scripture say something about helping the widows?" he said, biting his lip, while a grin seemed sure to burst forth.

RHONDA CRONKHITE

"Oh..." I said, nodding my head slowly. "So you make a point of helping the widows. Hmm...I see."

"Well actually, I'm just getting the revelation," he countered, his eyes now dancing. "But I'm sorry, Maggie. Please forgive me. I didn't mean to make light of your situation. I'm sure that being a widow is every bit as difficult as being a widower. And that's no picnic."

"That's okay, Peter. If we didn't joke once in a while, we'd soon be old withered up prunes, wouldn't we? What's it been now, about three years that you've been on your own? I was so sorry for you when you lost Sandi."

His smile faded as he looked off into the distance, biting his upper lip. When he looked back at me, I recognized the sadness in his eyes. "Yes, it's been a little over three years. Three pretty long years."

"I remember. It was as if you'd lost your best friend. That's so nice to see, especially after being married thirty plus years."

I also remembered how focused he'd been on their two children and the grandchildren, who seemed to be the light of his life. A great wave of compassion swept through my heart for this man. He obviously needed a diversion from the constant bleeding of his broken heart and to find some purpose to his life.

"Do you mind talking about it, Peter?" I asked softly. "I guess I've never asked you about what really happened, how you found out."

He looked at me, and then lowered his gaze, his

eyes searching for a focal point.

"It's okay if you don't want to talk about it. I understand, Peter. I didn't mean to be insensitive."

"No...no, it's okay. I don't talk about it much. It seems that after the first month or so, folks think you're doing better because you're not falling apart, at least in public, and they quit asking how you are. It's almost as if her memory faded along with the passing days. Or that's how it seems to feel. But then you know about that, don't you?"

"Mm hmm...yeah, that's how it feels," I murmured.

"When the hospital called to tell me there'd been an accident, I was terrified. Suddenly, I was in the middle of a nightmare, and I couldn't wake up. It was as if I was watching myself rushing to the hospital while everyone around me seemed to be in another dimension, totally unaffected by the awful tragedy that was ripping my world apart. I hurried to the emergency room, glancing around as I went in. I don't know what I was expecting, perhaps that she'd be sitting in a chair, waiting for me. The fear must have been written on my face because a nurse looked at me strangely and asked if she could help.

"As soon as I told her who I was, she told me to come right over and have a seat while she got the doctor.

"I sat down, my stomach in knots. Then I stood right back up, and started pacing back and forth, staring blindly in front of me. The next thing I knew, the doctor was there, saying he was sorry, that there was nothing they could do.

RHONDA CRONKHITE

"It felt like the room started spinning. I couldn't believe what I was hearing. Surely he didn't mean she was dead! I'd just seen her a couple of hours earlier. I figured there must be some mistake.

"It was as if the floor was jerked from under me, leaving me hanging in space, dizzy from the room's spinning. The walls seemed to be closing in, and someone was squeezing the breath out of me at the same time. It felt like I was drifting away from everyone, their voices becoming fainter, almost unrecognizable. *What was happening? Maybe I was going to die, too,* I thought. Then Zeke was there, asking me if I was okay...asking what had happened.

"I tried to tell him, but I couldn't even speak, nothing would come out when I moved my mouth. I started to cry and he realized she was gone. We clung to each other, sobbing together.

"You know, right after," his voice faltered, "I didn't know how I'd ever go on. The kids were good. They invited me often and that helped, but in the end, I still had to go home to an empty house and everywhere I looked, there was something that reminded me of her. I couldn't imagine life ever feeling right again." He paused, taking out his handkerchief and wiping his eyes. I heard the catch in his voice as he finished, "It was close to a year before I knew I'd be okay."

"I'm sorry, Peter," I murmured, my voice trembling, as I reached over, putting my hand on his arm. "I'm so sorry."

He nodded. "I remember when your Sam was

drowned, and you were there watching. I thought how awful that must have been. But I think I'd rather be there. It's a terrible shock hearing something like that."

My heart ached for him. *Poor Peter!* I wiped my eyes with my fingers, sniffling. "Oh, I agree" I said. I'd thought about that many times. "I've always been glad I was there. If I hadn't been, I'd have probably found someone to blame. After all, how could someone drown with that many people around?

"What has always tormented me though is not being able to say good-bye. It doesn't change what happened, but it would have been a small comfort and one less thing to deal with in the grieving process. I didn't get a chance with Sam or Amos. Or with my Mom either. But you know about that, too. It's just one of the things we have to accept, or go crazy thinking about."

"Oh, my! It's almost five o'clock," Peter exclaimed, looking at his watch. "I'm going to Kendra's for supper. I'd best be on my way." He rose and passed me his glass. "It was nice talking to you, Maggie. Thanks for the lemonade and for asking about Sandi. I still miss her...and I still weep sometimes. But it felt good to share with you. I guess it helps when someone understands.

"It doesn't seem fair, in a way," he continued, "how we have to go on living without them, to make a new path for ourselves, a path where they're just beautiful memories."

I understood completely.

RHONDA CRONKHITE

"How do you like my little room, Peter?" I asked, wanting to leave the conversation on a happier note.

"I think it's quite charming, actually," he said, looking around thoughtfully. "I noticed those fancy doors. Where did you get those?"

"Oh, Sebastian painted those when he was fifteen. They were his closet doors. I don't call myself a sentimental old fool for no reason," I said playfully. "I took them, figuring I'd find a use for them somewhere. I sprayed them with several coats of exterior varnish, and voila! I think they make a rather lovely addition to my masterpiece."

"It looks like you have a good imagination, Maggie. That can keep one from getting bored."

"I think you're right there. I don't know much about being bored." I glanced around at the gardens where I spend most of my summers. I joke that what my cottage lacks in size and style, the view of the river and my gardens makes up for.

My place is a small one-bedroom house, christened 'the cottage.' I grew up on this property in what we called *The Little Red House*. We named all of our houses, and this one was special. It was the only house Dad ever owned, but he sold it to be handy his work. His theory had always been that *a rolling stone gathers no moss*, and I can't say that I disagree. He never did seem to get too green. It was a coincidence that he and Mom moved back here as tenants. Amos and I decided to buy it, definitely influenced by my sentimentality.

The original house had burned at some point, and

another little red house was built. We painted the trim yellow and the doors a deep purple. The nicest thing about the house is the little deck Amos built on the front. The side steps go out to the driveway, with patio stones that Amos wouldn't hear of placing without using his level. Purple thyme fills in the spaces between the stones. I wanted steps on the other side, too, so I could make a path to the brook. Amos decided he wanted to recess them, at an angle.

We had built a little deck on the back, with a ramp going the length of the house for Mom, who had lost a leg and needed a wheelchair, and now it comes in handy for my son, Luke, since he's in a wheelchair.

Right beside this deck is the wall I've made where my sentimental doors are hanging. Pink and purple wisteria, growing on a vegetable trellis, fills in the space on either side of the doors, making a wall to meet the silver maple. The other silver maple is in line with the front of the house. There, a wall of red and yellow climbing roses forms the front of my little room.

The room has only three sides. A hammock hangs between the silver maples with lamian and dew drops growing underneath. It's a cozy retreat on a warm afternoon.

I walked with Peter to his truck. "Thank you so much for the help, and for sharing your story with me."

"Glad I could help," he replied, his hazel eyes twinkling.

I watched as he climbed up into his truck. It was

white with 'Weatherburn Trucking' and his phone number painted in red letters on the door. The dump was red with "At Your Service" painted in white italics. *Cute. Isn't that what he'd said to me?* As he put the truck in reverse, his eyes were twinkling as he said "See you around."

I found myself already wondering just when that would be. I'd always known that Peter was a nice fellow, full of fun, and a soft-spoken family man. *Well, I could sure use some of that!* Waving as he went, I silently chided myself for letting my thoughts tear around like a silly schoolgirl.

Chapter 2

Peter Calls

I WAS HEADING OUT to do some gardening when the phone rang. *Now who can that be?* "Hello-o," I answered, anxious to be on my way. The soil was calling me.

"Hello Maggie. It's Peter. I'm taking some vegetables to Bennington and wondered if you'd like to come along for the drive."

"Oh Peter, it's you," I exclaimed, unable to keep the excitement from my voice. "I'd love that. I'll be ready when you get here." *My gardening can wait!* I would enjoy seeing Peter again. I'd found myself reliving his visit many times over the last couple of weeks.

Twenty minutes later, I answered his light knock. Flashing his disarming smile, he said, "I'm glad you could come on such short notice."

I looked at him standing there. He was strikingly handsome, and either didn't know it, or didn't care, dark blond curls falling carelessly on his forehead, his cap in his hand. I've been accused of being too serious.

When I first met Sam, my grandmother had remarked, "It's nice to see you smile, Maggie." It was equally as easy to smile at the sight of Peter Weatherburn.

My pulse quickened. "Well, I don't exactly have a lot of commitments these days. And the thing I've noticed about work is that it's never in a hurry, nor does it ever leave without you," I joshed, rolling my eyes and chuckling. "It's always waiting right where you left it. I think a nice drive beats working any day. Would you care for a drink while I'm finishing up? I won't be long."

"Sure, that sounds good," he said, as we went into the kitchen, his eyes following me as I got a glass and went to the fridge.

"You're looking pretty today, Maggie," he said softly, without smiling, but his eyes seemed to be saying things that made me feel sure there were butterflies in my chest.

I stopped and looked at him, letting my eyes respond to what his had given away. "Thank you so much, Prince Charming. As long as I look good enough to go driving with you, I'm happy with that."

A hint of pink crept above his collar. "Oh, you do," he said, a little gleam crinkling his eyes.

As we were heading out the door, he asked, "Are you bringing those three musketeers? I think we have room for them. They seem to be keeping a pretty close eye on you, and I notice they don't let you get very far away."

RHONDA CRONKHITE

"Yes, let's," I agreed and grabbed some treats and a blanket, as three very happy little dogs wagged their tails, rushing excitedly out the door ahead of us.

"All set?" Peter asked, when we had the dogs settled.

"We're all ready."

The time went by quickly with Peter talking about his work and me musing aloud about my semi-retirement while we finished off a bag of toasted coconut marshmallows that was lying on the seat.

After the load was delivered, we decided to grab a bite to eat at a restaurant nearby. I ordered a chicken sandwich and tea and started to reach in my purse. "I'll get it," Peter said. "I invited you."

"So that's how it works, is it?" I said, smiling. "I'll remember that. It is 2012, though, you know."

"So it is," was his reply.

It was quiet at first as we headed back. Cinnamon was sleeping on my lap, Kiwi asleep on the seat between us, and Cookie snuggled up on a blanket on the floor.

"Tell me about your children, Peter. I'd have had a house full of them if the choice had been mine."

Glancing at me with raised eyebrows, he said, "They are pretty special, aren't they? But a house full? I don't think many women would say that," he chuckled softly. "Zeke is thirty-eight. He's been the administrator at the nursing home for eight years. He and Ruby have been married, let's see, they got married when Zeke was twenty-two, so sixteen years, I guess. They live in Hanover.

"They have a son, Peter, he's fourteen. We call him Pete. Liz is eleven. She's named after Mom. Her middle name was Elizabeth. Ruby is a nurse but she's chosen to stay at home, at least while the children are young.

"Kendra and Arnie live in Enfield, a couple of miles from my place. They're both thirty-two. They have two kids, Ben is four and Marissa is six. Arnie is an accountant and Kendra has started an online business. It's taken her awhile, but she's worked hard at it. She tells me she's about ready to launch her first website, whatever that entails," he said, shrugging his shoulders and laughing softly. "She has a site on natural remedies, I think it's called *Healing From Home.* She's written a book about it. We're pretty proud of her, and hope she does well with it."

"That's brilliant," I said. "You deserve to be proud. It's nice that she'll be able to work and be with the children, too."

All too soon, we were back. "I enjoyed the day, Maggie," Peter said. "You make life seem fun again. I've always admired you...from a distance, of course. You seem to have been a strong woman, but there's another side to you, I'm seeing."

"I don't know about that," I chuckled. "I've just learned that when life throws a curve ball and knocks you down, you'd best get up, dust yourself off, and get going again. Another thing I decided a long time ago is that my cup is half full. There's no sense in sitting around moaning, 'why me?'"

"Well, you've survived, and don't look any worse for the wear," he teased.

"You can't always judge a book by its cover, you know," I laughed.

"The cover looks just fine to me. And what I've seen, from a distance, at least, seems quite remarkable. You were so young when Sam drowned, I can't imagine what that must have been like. You raised Luke by yourself, and stood by Amos through his rough times. That couldn't have been easy, but it was obvious that your support made a big difference in his life. I think at least the summary of the book looks pretty good."

"You're a character, Peter!" I said. "You're flattering me. I just did what seemed natural. I certainly didn't feel strong after Sam was drowned. I lived in a fog for a year, drifting here and there, like I didn't belong anywhere.

"I'm real big on treating others as I'd want to be treated, too. When it's all said and done, I'm very glad that I could help Amos." I paused. "He was really different the last few years," I said, thinking for a moment about his patience during my rough times. "He was wonderful when I was stressed out at work and I'd come down to stay with him for a few days.

"After Luke was hurt, things were really tough. Luke and his girlfriend had been my main support at the special care home, and when I lost their help, it seemed like my load tripled. I almost collapsed." Giggling, I went on, "Well, maybe it was more than 'almost.' Thoughts of that long night when I'd heard that Luke had fallen from a tree flashed through my mind. Life had certainly changed after that.

"There was one particular night," I continued, picking up where I'd left off, "that gave me a scare. It was midnight by the time I was able to get away and for some reason, I came into town on a different route. When I got to the road I usually took to get here, I missed it and ended up crossing the bridge. I was disoriented and didn't know how to get back. I had Sebastian's cell phone because he'd taken mine to Arizona. I couldn't get it working right and I panicked."

Peter was leaning toward me, listening intently.

"I finally got through to Amos and he calmed me down some, but I was still nervous. He told me to stay right where I was and he'd come and get me. I did manage to get turned around and headed up our road, but he made me feel very safe. As I've thought about it since, it doesn't make any sense. Why didn't I just turn around in the first place?

"When I was here, I slept a lot. I didn't even get dressed most days. When he knew I was coming, he'd ask what I wanted to eat and have a meal ready when I got here. It felt really good to have someone looking after me during that period of my life.

"The last year, though, he was so sick. He suffered so much and I have a lot of guilty feelings. I know I did the best I could do with the load I was carrying, but it wasn't enough.

"You know, Peter, you're quite amazing yourself. I've never met anyone quite like you. You seem so comfortable with yourself and you get along with everyone. Do you ever get upset?"

He laughed. "I try not to, but if something eats at me long enough, I find a way to address it. Being angry takes a lot of energy and I've never noticed much accomplished by it."

The dogs were starting to whimper, with Cookie pacing back and forth to the door, so I let them out. "It was a lovely afternoon, Peter. I enjoyed your company, too."

My heart was light as he saw me to the door.

Chapter 3

Stopping By

PETER STOPPED BY ONE AFTERNOON to see if I'd like to go to Northampton with him. He was delivering french fries to Big Y Foods. It was just a short drive and he'd be gone an hour and a half.

I was already smitten with Peter. Just seeing him set my heart aflutter, let alone when he smiled at me, almost tenderly. I suspected that 'tenderly' was just natural to Peter, so maybe it didn't mean as much as I wanted it to. Regardless, it made me a little giddy. I fixed my hair, grabbed a couple of snacks and drinks, and was ready.

On the way back, I turned towards him, curled one leg underneath myself and settled in for a comfortable ride.

"Tell me something about yourself, Peter, something I don't know. Which could be a lot, I suppose."

"What would you like to know?" he asked.

"Oh, what you do in your spare time, what your favorite food is, just anything."

"My favourite food? I don't know, I just love to eat.

The one thing I can't do without, though, is molasses. Breakfast, dinner, or supper, it doesn't matter. I just keep the jar on the table now. There's no one to tell me I can't, eh," he chuckled, casting a sidelong glance in my direction.

"I spend a lot of time with my kids. They each have me over for a meal every week. On Sundays, after church, we go out somewhere for dinner. On Sunday evenings, they all drop by and I usually have a pie, from the bakery, of course, and we just hang out.

"Sometimes I visit my friend, Judah, and he drops by once in a while. They often invite me for a meal, too, but I don't return the favour. I don't think I want to get into preparing full course meals. I can throw something together for myself, but there's no inspectors around, eh" he said. "I guess I keep pretty busy."

I had to pinch myself to be sure I wasn't dreaming, sitting so comfortable, next to Peter, and feeling so at ease.

Goodness, I couldn't believe we were back already. Where did the time go?

"I'm barbecuing for supper. Would you like to join me?" I asked, as we were pulling into the driveway.

"I'd love that, Maggie."

As I hurried inside to get things going, Peter asked if there was anything he could do to help.

"You could start the barbecue. There's hotdogs and hamburger in the fridge and the barbecue sauce is in the fridge door. I'm going to put some onions on to fry."

He got the meat and sauce and went out to get started. When I had the onions cooking, I buttered some buns and made some Kool-Aid. I put the condiments on a tray, along with the onions, now done to perfection, and took them out to the table.

The picnic table is in the picnic room between the back deck and the greenhouse. I love the little greenhouse Amos built for me. We'd carried windows around for years, hoping to build one someday and he'd finally found the time to do it.

Paths lead everywhere, made with different kinds of patio blocks, making it easier for Luke to get around in his wheelchair. He loves gardens and had always helped me, digging holes, chopping roots out, just having fun like I do. We loved picking berries, learning to leave Amos at home so he'd be in a fit frame of mind to dig into them when we returned.

Sebastian, my eldest grandson, shared my enthusiasm for gardening and berry picking from the time he was two years old. His younger brother, Nicholas, however, never had much use for either and certainly adopted Poppy's theory that berries taste much better when there's no work involved. I took him to help pick raspberries once and vowed I wouldn't take him again. He complained the whole time, tormenting Sebastian, and eating almost as many berries as he picked. It was a disaster, but maybe that was his plan.

The areas around the walks have a few shrubs and small evergreens, filled in with different sizes of crushed rock. One of these paths leads to the greenhouse. Beside it, on the upper side, is the picnic room, sitting on patio stones, with four-foot brick walls on three sides, leaving the side facing the walkway open.

The structure actually has two rooms with the barbecue in the smaller one. On the far wall is the bar sink that Luke gave me from one of his renovation jobs. Like Sebastian's doors, I'd kept it, knowing I'd find a use for it someday. A shelf above the sink holds an old clock shaped like a house.

The three-foot wall between the rooms makes it easy for passing food over. Three eight by eights extend up from the back wall, with shorter ones lag bolted on, going out to the front of the room. Several umbrellas, attached at different angles, acts as a roof of sorts.

In the larger room, along with the table and chairs, there's a small cupboard that I painted yellow, matching the house trim. I keep a supply of paper products and picnic utensils in it, along with a couple of tablecloths and the barbecue lighter.

I lit the candles sitting on the cupboard and threw down the tablecloth that Uncle Jack had brought back from overseas. It proudly displayed the emblems of several countries. We were soon eating in comfortable silence, enjoying the blue jay chirping in the nearby beech tree while two hummingbirds fluttered around the feeder at the back step.

"You've created quite a garden here, Maggie. It looks like something you'd read about in a book."

"Yeah? Thank you. I get a lot of enjoyment playing out here. I do get some ideas from magazines, and some I just dream up. Painting the greenhouse with a half-tint of the house colour was something I saw in a gardening magazine. They'd also used an accent colour to paint some lawn ornaments and furniture, so I did that, too. I'm quite pleased with it."

When we finished eating, I suggested we take a walk out front, I suppose so I could show off what I'd done out there. I was somewhat enjoying the attention being lavished on all my hard work.

We started down the path next to the silver maple room. The row of shrubs on the right were in various stages of bloom, the honeysuckle and rose I'd taken from Sam's mother's garden among my favourites.

We crossed the black stone path going from the upper patio steps to the brook. Tiny step-on-me plants growing between the stones still allows Luke to go there in his power chair. It's too steep for his regular chair.

The lighthouse Amos bought me, surrounded by huge rocks I'd gathered, sits beside the path, beckoning me, its light reminding me that all is well and I am forgiven. I buried the cord leading to it after accidentally cutting it off with the mower. I am, unfortunately, famous for being absent minded...

We meandered on through the crisscrossing paths separating the gardens, enjoying the sweet scent of the honeysuckle and magnolia. Several Japanese maple and pink crepe myrtles added contrast to the lighter colours. I love the little alcove Amos made with sections of trellis, hanging a lantern on the framework. Peter and I sat down on the bench there.

As dusk was gathering, the frogs began their evening chorus, their voices floating up from the brook as the warm evening breeze rustled the leaves of the flowering crab in the bed across from us. The tiny lights I'd strung through the branches cast soft dancing shadows, creating a magical atmosphere.

The moon was high in the sky when Peter decided it was time he set out for home.. The spell was broken only momentarily - until he gave me his hand, helping me up. As we started towards his truck, I was delighted when he kept my hand in his. I couldn't resist picking a few blue asters as we passed in front of the house.

"I'm glad you asked me to go with you today, Peter. I enjoyed it. And it was nice you could stay for supper, too. You're pretty good company, you know," I said, smiling my pleasure.

"I enjoyed it too, Maggie. I'm glad you could come with me. It was nice having supper with you and spending the evening." Holding my gaze for so long that my heart started misbehaving, he said softly, "It was lovely, Maggie."

After thinking for a moment, he said, "I don't have anything planned for Saturday. Would you like to go out for supper?"

I hesitated for a second. *That sounds like a real date.* "Actually, my sister, Sherry, is singing at the gospel concert Saturday evening and I was planning to go. I'd love to have company though," I said, hesitantly. "Why don't you come with me? I could drive up and meet you and we could have something quick to eat before the concert."

"Okay. How about I call you tomorrow night and we can decide where to meet?"

When he left, I took the dishes inside. I was surprised at how empty and lonely I suddenly felt with Peter gone. *Wow! I guess I really am hooked.*

Chapter 4

Zeke and Ruby

BEFORE MEETING PETER ON SATURDAY, I spent a leisurely afternoon, stopping at Luke's and then going for a spa treatment. After all, I wanted to look my best for our first official date - at least I hoped it was. We found a cozy little restaurant where we enjoyed a lovely meal and easy laughter.

When supper was finished, Peter asked if I'd like to drop by and see his son Zeke, and Zeke's wife, Ruby. It was just a few minutes to their place. Although I was a bit nervous, I agreed. I had met his son a couple of times over the years, and he seemed like a well-rounded young man. I convinced myself this would be a casual meeting after all, just his Dad and a friend, nothing for him to worry about.

When we drove in, Zeke was getting out of his car. He is the spitting image of his dad, but a few inches taller than Peter's five feet, ten inches, and has apparently inherited, or picked up, his Dad's teasing nature.

His eyes twinkled with merriment as a big smile spread across his face. "So this is the lovely lady

Dad's been raving about. I'm pleased to meet you, Maggie," he said, reaching to shake my hand.

Was Peter embarrassed? "Zeke! Didn't your mother teach you not to tell tales out of school?" Peter said, looking as if he'd just been squealed on.

"Oh, did she? I forgot for a moment," Zeke said with a guilty looking smirk. "Come on in and have something to drink. Ruby will be glad to meet you."

Ruby's eyes were warm as she gave me a little hug. "It's such a pleasure to meet you, Maggie." She was slim, a little shorter than Zeke, her blond curly hair tied back with a scarf.

We had a cup of coffee with chocolate coconut macaroons that Ruby had just finished making - one of Peter's favourites, she said. *I'll have to remember that.* I had noticed that Ruby had some gardens so it wasn't hard to keep the conversation going.

"Maggie practically lives in her gardens," Peter said. "You might even catch her sleeping there."

"Yes, I do," I agreed, "spend lots of time, that is. I don't have time to sleep. I'll have you over sometime, Ruby. We might be able to swap some things."

Ruby laughed. "Oh, I'd like that. I can't ever seem to get enough plants. Sometimes it's hard to find room for them, but they end up fitting in. Then the next time I see something on sale, I want that, too."

"Oh, I understand that," I said.

The visit was going much easier than I had envisioned. Zeke and Ruby both seemed relaxed. The time passed quickly and before I knew it, Peter was saying, "We're going to a concert at seven o'clock. We thought we'd stop by for a few minutes." Rising to leave, he said, "I'll see you guys tomorrow night."

"Sure thing, Dad" Ruby said, smiling lovingly at Peter. It was obvious that her father-in-law was pretty special.

Walking with us to the car, Zeke put his arm around his dad. "I love you Dad. I'm not sure what Mom told me, but I do recall my dad teaching me what fun it is to tease."

"Okay, okay. I guess you're right," Peter agreed. "I'll live, Son. No need to worry."

I smiled at them both.

On the way to the concert, I told Peter how much I'd enjoyed meeting Zeke and Ruby. "They're lovely. I like them."

"Thank you," he said. "I'm glad you like them. We're all a pretty easy-going bunch. No airs. What you see is what you get."

"Uh huh" I murmured. *Well, I like what I see so far*.

"My family has always been special to me," Peter continued. "When we were growing up, we always knew Dad loved us, but he was too busy to do things with us. Sometimes he'd take me to town with him but I'd have liked to do some of the fun things like other kids did with their dads.

"Before we even had kids, I decided I was going to take the time to teach my children to fish, pick fiddle-heads and work in the garden together; all the things I missed. We enjoyed it, or at least I did," he said, with a little laugh.

"I know we all plan to have ideal families but it takes a lot more effort than we think when we're young and seeing all the faults in everyone else's.

"The other thing I said was that I might not be as tough on my children as I'd seen others being. I think sometimes parents are so strict that the kids aren't allowed to be kids. I said that mine might get off with quite a lot, but, when I spoke, I intended for them to know that I wasn't fooling; and that's what I did, much to the disapproval of others, I'm sure.

"I've always tried to live by my own convictions, which I take seriously. I don't take too well to someone else telling me how to do things. I guess that's just the way I am," he finished.

"I like that in a person," I said, nodding my approval.

The crowd was starting to gather when we arrived at The Salvation Army. I'd been there a few times alone since Amos had been gone. Sherry was setting up a table with her CDs. She asked if Peter and I would mind helping her handle customers at intermission.

We found a seat not too far from the back where we had a good view. I was happy to see Gracie Jackson sitting a couple of seats ahead of us. We'd met at an event a year ago. She's very outgoing and had started talking to me like an old friend. I had been alone that evening, and she was great company.

As Peter and I were getting seated, she turned

around, smiling when she saw me. When she noticed Peter, her eyes lit up. She turned back around, but her curiosity must have gotten the better of her. She was soon on her way back asking who the lucky man was.

The concert was soon under way with Blake Oliver as the first artist. Blake is an older gentleman who sings old fashioned country gospel, the way I like it, with feeling. He even sang my favourite, "Another Brand New Day."

When Sherry's turn came, the crowd was applauding before she even got started. Her down to earth country goodness is what makes her special. There's no putting on airs, she just sings the way she feels. Someone requested "If You Only Knew," a song she put on one of her albums in memory of Mom. I had her sing it at Amos' service, too.

It was another treat when The Revivalists sang. Gracie's husband, Hank, heads the group. He was a preacher's kid back when we were teenagers. He was a nice boy who didn't act stuck up because his dad was the preacher. He's still as handsome as ever, and as nice. The only difference is that now I speak to him. Back then, I was too shy. I've asked him when he's going to sing "Jesus" for me, but he doesn't act like it's in his plans. Oh, well!

I love the lead singer, Cody Robbins, too. He has a beautiful voice, and gets right into his singing. He looks so much like Sebastian that it's uncanny. The first time I heard him sing, I couldn't take my eyes off him, it was like I was watching Sebastian on the stage. They even combed their hair the same, and wore the same glasses. I decided to take a picture, but was having trouble with the camera. A little embarrassed, but too old to really care, I finally got it. I told him afterwards why I was trying to get his picture. "You don't look old enough to be my grandmother," he said.

"Oh, but I am." I answered. He made my day.

Peter watched with amusement as I clapped my hands, moving back and forth to the music, or tapping my feet. "You're having a ball, aren't you?" he said.

I'll admit I was feeling pretty happy. "That's not too hard when you have the most charming man in the audience sitting beside you."

"I think it's the other way around," he countered. "I've been looking around, and I think my seat is the best." He has so many ways of making my heart act all crazy. I didn't say anything, but tucked the little comment away to think about later.

I met several friends and some cousins, proudly introducing Peter to them. They were surprised, and I knew they were thrilled for me. My cousin, Charlene, whispered, "I'm happy for you, Maggie." I'm sure my glowing face told how I felt.

After the concert, Peter asked if I'd like to get a coffee.

"On one condition," was my reply.

"And what would that be?"

"I'm buying."

"But, I..." he began.

"You bought supper. The concert was my idea, so it's my treat. What do you say?" I raised my eyebrows in question, waiting for an answer.

"Oh, come on," he said, linking my arm in his.

Chapter 5

Luke

WE WERE SITTING OUTSIDE, enjoying the cool evening breeze when we heard a car on the drive. It was Luke, stopping by on his way back from visiting his friend, Jonathan. He smiled as we walked over.

"Hi, Luke," I said. "You remember Peter, don't you? We've seen him at church sometimes."

"Yes, I do remember him. Nice to see you again, Peter." His eyes said, 'Yes, Mom. You mean the man I've been hearing so much about.' *At least he didn't say it out loud.*

"It's nice to see you, too, Luke. You're looking good."

"Would you like to get out and have something to drink with us?" I asked.

"That would be nice, if it's not too much trouble, Ma."

I got his wheelchair from the back seat and the wheels from the trunk, put it together, and helped him out of the car. He wheeled over to where we were sitting on the gravel next to the picnic room, while I went inside and got him a glass of his favourite orange juice.

Luke is handsome with brown hair that wants to curl when it gets a little length to it, sparkling hazel eyes, and a smile that can melt your heart. He's six feet tall but says he shrunk to four feet overnight. That was after the fall that left him paralyzed, a quadriplegic. But he is fortunate because he can move his arms and wrists. He's actually surpassed all expectations the doctors had given him hope for. Being able to drive has given him some independence.

"It looks like you're doing very well, Luke," Peter said. "Your mom is sure proud of you. Says you've worked really hard, and I guess it shows."

"I've tried to work hard. I realized that's the only way I'd have any quality of life at all. And it's been worth it. Maybe I get my determination from Mom."

"It must have been a very difficult situation to come to terms with," Peter said, slowly shaking his head.

"You can say that again!" Luke agreed. "Every day is a new day, and I try to stay positive. Kate's been a big encouragement to me."

"Your mom was telling me about you getting married. She seems to think a lot of Kate."

"Yes. It seems to be a two-way street," Luke replied, laughing lightly, "and I guess that's very lucky for me." He and Peter chatted easily, while I did most of the listening. Luke has more of his dad's easy-going nature than the LaHaye brusqueness, thank goodness.

I always love to see him come and hate to see him leave. Even with Peter there, I felt a twinge of nostalgia as he left.

"You've got a charming son there, Maggie," Peter said. "It looks like you've done a good job."

"Thank you, Peter. I certainly tried, but looking back, I'd definitely do some things differently. I was so young and alone. I was very hard on him in some ways, but he always knew where his mother was and that there would be a meal on the table. Even though our life seemed a bit chaotic at times, I tried to make things feel as normal as I could.

"He and Amos had a lot of difficulties and I was caught in the middle. They'd made up before Luke was hurt, and that was a huge blessing. You can imagine what that did for me."

Peter nodded.

"He was just getting the chance to do so many things that he enjoyed. He'd got his first deer just the year before. I think the deer thought several hunters had moved to the area and not just one inexperienced one. He had upgraded his diving certificate, got a motorbike, put a snow plow on his truck and was really enjoying it all.

"The way he's taken it, though, has amazed me. He's been so strong and determined. He's very easygoing, like his dad. Sometimes he reminds me a lot of Sam. Sam would be proud of him."

Chapter 6

Calling?

ON A SUNNY MORNING, AS I WAS WAITING for Peter to arrive, my thoughts drifted back over the past few weeks. Life had been so much different since the day Peter Weatherburn had driven in my yard. I'd found myself looking forward to his calls and visits.

Hearing his knock, I rushed to the door, opening it to find him holding a bouquet of dark pink lilies with lily of the valley mixed in among them. With a straight face and just a slight twinkling of his beautiful eyes, he asked, "I wondered if I could come calling?" He reminded me of a shy schoolboy.

My heart raced. Peter looked younger than his years and although he had gained a few pounds, it wasn't close to the twenty-five I had gained. He cut a pretty nice picture, but more than that, he was pretty nice, himself. I already knew he cared for me, but this was another step and I was excited to take it.

"Oh Peter, they're lovely," I cried, taking the bouquet and burying my face in their sweetness, trying to quiet the butterflies doing the polka in my chest. "Thank you so much." I was sure my face was glowing. "I'd be delighted to have you come calling, Peter. I can't think of another man I'd sooner open my door to. But do come in, I'm so excited about the flowers, I've left you standing outside."

"I'm pleased you like them," he said, smiling his pleasure.

"They're adorable, Peter, but I like their intent even better," I said, hearing the unabashed delight in my voice.

"What do you say we do something special, then? To celebrate. We could go to the Fair, or I heard that the Booth Brothers are having a concert in Houlton. It's a long drive, but we have lots of time. Unless you have a curfew, of course." I didn't miss the teasing glint in his eyes.

"Oh, that's a splendid idea. The concert. I wouldn't turn down a chance to hear the Booth Brothers. They're my favourite male group." The long drive would just be an added bonus. *I can handle that.*

As we headed out, I said, "You mentioned curfews earlier. When we were teenagers, curfews weren't our problem. It was the tests my parents required the young man to pass before we were allowed to go out with him. Pretty stiff tests, we thought, but if the fellow was lucky enough to pass those, it didn't matter whether we came in at ten o'clock, or two o'clock. It wasn't just the boys, though. Our girl friends were analyzed and scrutinized to the same degree, much to our dismay."

The time flew by quickly, sometimes in comfortable silence, sometimes with Peter singing softly, not at all bothered when his voice strayed from the tune. I knew he wouldn't be competing with the Booth Brothers, but his sincerity matched theirs.

The concert was fantastic, as I knew it would be. The Booth Brothers have won several awards. Someone said if you don't think males can sing softly, you haven't heard the Booth Brothers. The first song I ever heard them sing spoke to me. I was going through some tough stuff and when I heard, "I'm Still Feeling Fine," it quickly became one of my favourites. I was impressed when they said that if anyone wanted a CD and didn't have the money, to take one anyway.

We stopped for coffee and a quick bite to eat. There was silence after we'd placed our orders. When I looked at Peter, he was studying me intently. My heart fluttered as I met his gaze, and he reached over, putting his hand over mine. I think my heart stopped then, gathering momentum to jump into my throat. I couldn't speak for a moment. I hadn't noticed how perfect his hands were, the fingers straight and even, not big and knobby like my own. His nails were smooth and clean. On impulse, I decided to just be honest. "I..I feel like a teenager. I'm nervous all of a sudden," I stuttered, feeling the colour rising in my cheeks.

I closed my eyes for a moment. *Why should I feel so flustered?* Looking at Peter, I said softly, "You *are* charming, Peter." I couldn't miss the sparkle in his eyes and the contented look on his face.

Later, at my door, he took my hand, looking at me with what I recognized as the stirrings of young love. His voice was soft as he said, "I've enjoyed spending time with you these last few weeks, getting to know you better. You're a pretty special lady, Maggie."

"Thank you, Peter," I replied softly, matching the soft purring of my heart. "I've enjoyed every minute of it. You're pretty special yourself."

He kissed me lightly on the forehead. Squeezing my hand, he whispered, "See you soon, Maggie. Good night." I watched as he slowly retreated to his vehicle, his shoulders drooping.

"Goodnight, Peter. Drive safely."

Later, I couldn't sleep as I kept replaying the events of the evening. My life was changing so fast, but I loved it. I felt very special to have the attentions of Peter Weatherburn; he was a man of integrity and honour.

It had only been a few weeks since he stopped in that day, but it felt like we were meant to be together. I could tell that he admired me for the woman I was, while his heart was telling him that he wanted me for his own. The way he looked at me set my heart to racing. *Well, I'll just have to watch the drama unfold and enjoy being one of the stars.*

Chapter 7

Peter's Family

THE DAY DAWNED BRIGHT AND SUNNY and I was quite excited to be going to Zeke's home for a potluck. Kendra and Arnie would be there along with their children, too. I was taking cabbage rolls, baked beans, and some air buns. I love to have a reason to cook.

When Peter arrived shortly after noon, he was surprised at the food I'd prepared. "You didn't need to go to all that trouble, Maggie," he said.

"I'm so excited to be meeting your family that I guess I got carried away. And I do love to cook. If your clan eats anything like mine, there can never be too much food."

When we arrived, Zeke and Ruby came out to meet us, arm in arm. They really were a handsome couple. Their children, Pete, tall and blond, and Liz, with blond curly hair like her mother's, were bringing the paper plates and utensils outside.

Kendra and Arnie were just arriving. Kendra looked about five feet tall, very slim, with strawberry blond permed hair. She got busy getting her food arranged, barely glancing in my direction. When

Ruby introduced me, she nodded and mumbled, "Hello, Maggie." Her husband, Arnie, is about six inches taller with red hair that he wears slicked back. Their daughter, Marissa, six, with red hair lighter than her dad's, smiled shyly, and said "Hi, Maggie," lowering her head a little, while looking up at me. Their four-year-old son, Ben, has his mother's strawberry blond hair and freckles. He came running towards us and Peter quickly had him in his arms.

"How's Grampa's young man today?" Peter asked, the glow in his eyes revealing just what his grandkids mean to him.

"I'm good, Grampa, at least that's what you always say. Do you have any candy?"

"You'll have to check my pocket and see. It's hard to say," he teased, as Ben reached in his pocket and found two pink peppermints.

"Yay! I love those Grampa." Peter squeezed him tighter. "I know you pretty good, Ben."

We walked over to where Pete and Liz were getting the tables ready. "How's Grampa's big kids, today?" Peter asked, squeezing each one with his free arm. "Don't you think I have the bestest grandchildren ever, Maggie?" he asked, his pride bubbling over, as Ben decided he wanted down to see if he could help his cousins.

"They seem perfectly lovely to me, Peter." Looking him in the eye with a little smirk, I said, "They must take after their Grampa, do you suppose? Grandchildren are one of the nicest things that can happen to a person, aren't they?"

RHONDA CRONKHITE

His voice was even as he replied, "Yes, 'one' of the nicest things to be sure," giving me a little wink as a daring grin shot across his face.

I talked to Pete and Liz for a few minutes, asked about school, and offered to help set the tables. They looked uncertain as to what they should say. There were bottles of pickles; dill, mustard and pickled beets, sitting on a table with several small dishes, so I got those ready, while we continued chatting, me doing most of the talking. I remembered being that age and not knowing quite how to carry on a conversation, but feeling good inside when an older person talked to me like I just might be a grownup someday.

Everything was soon ready and Zeke asked his Dad to give thanks for the food. Peter nodded as we bowed our heads while he offered a simple prayer.

Ruby had made a potato scallop, baked rice, and brown rolls. Kendra brought stuffed cannelloni and a meat loaf. Everyone loved the cabbage rolls and baked beans. Baked beans are always a safe item for a potluck. There was fruit salad, pumpkin cookies and lemon squares for dessert.

Marissa was keeping an eye on me and as I headed inside to help with the cleanup, I called to her, "Hey, Marissa, let's go see if we can help Mommy and Aunt Ruby." Her face beaming, she came running to my side, taking my hand.

When the dishes were done, the ladies went back outside to join the men. They had the folding tables put away and were sitting around the fire pit. Ben strolled up to me. "Are you and Grampa friends?" he asked, his eyebrows knit together.

"Yes, we are friends, Ben," I said, feeling a little thrill at acknowledging that I was, indeed, his grampa's friend.

"I don't think Gramma would like it," he said, his expression glum.

"Why do you say that, Ben?" I asked, taken aback.

"Cuz. She'd be sad that Grampa doesn't love her anymore." Giving me a stern look, he went on, "Are you gonna be our new gramma?"

Tousling his hair, I said, "What makes you ask that?"

He stopped, squinting his eyes as he turned towards me, putting his hands on his hips and one foot ahead of the other. "Well, whadda ya think?" *Oh! Sounds like I'm in for it.* "Gramma used to come with Grampa. Then he came by himself. Now he's bringing you," he said, apparently annoyed at my inability to see the obvious.

Avoiding his question, I said, "I don't think your grampa would do anything to make your gramma sad, do you, Ben?"

"Well no-o-o," he answered, puckering his eyebrows as he looked at me, his eyes full of questions. "I don't think so." We walked in silence for a moment. "Why do you have a ring on? Grampa doesn't wear a ring. Are you married?" he asked.

"I was, Ben. I have a son about Uncle Zeke's age. His name is Luke. His dad died when Luke was little.

Later, I got married again and my husband died last year."

"Why do you wear a ring if you're not married?" he asked, with the frankness of a four-year-old. He was evidently determined to get to the bottom of his concerns.

Instinctively, I felt my hand, fingering my ring. "You're right, Ben. I guess I'm so used to wearing it that I don't even think about it." That was true but in the beginning I hadn't wanted people to think I was shopping and had purposely kept my public profile as "married." To Ben, I said, "I guess maybe I should put it in my jewellery box. What do you think?"

"Grampa doesn't wear his. People might think you and Grampa are married," he said, shaking his head slowly.

"You're right, Ben. I'm glad you noticed it. I'll take it off when I get home. How about that's our little secret? We won't tell anyone," I whispered. "What do you say, can you keep a secret?"

Puckering his mouth and squinting his eyes at me again, he said slowly, "I'm not supposed to keep secrets...but this one isn't bad so I think maybe I can. I think it will be alright."

"I won't tell if you don't," I whispered. *Quite the interrogation! Did I make a little progress?*

Later, we were riding quietly, each lost in our own thoughts. "It was nice having you along today, Maggie. I think you made a pretty good impression, too," Peter said.

"You have a lovely family, Peter. I like them. It must be difficult for kids, even grown ones, to see their parent with someone else. They made me feel welcome, though."

"Kendra was quite impressed when you asked about her mother. She said that so many times she's wanted to ask her mom about things, like cooking, or something with the kids. She was surprised when you mentioned that she must miss her mom and how much a young woman needs her mother. She was quite touched by that."

"I guess my own trials have blessed me with a lot of empathy for others," I said, thoughtfully. "I enjoyed myself a lot. It was a really nice day."

Later that evening, as I got ready for bed, I went to my jewellery box, taking my wedding rings off and turning them thoughtfully, memories of other days flitting through my mind. *Goodness, what must Peter have thought with me still wearing Amos' rings!* Laying them carefully in the box, I thought I should get the little case they came in and put both mine and Amos' in it. *Perhaps I'll put them in the memory bag I've kept in my nightstand.* I realized I hadn't taken it out and looked through it lately. I would again, though, I was sure.

Chapter 8

Peter's Place

I WAS GOING TO SEE MY DOCTOR in White River Junction and Peter asked if I'd like to come by for coffee. After my appointment, I stopped at the doughnut shop and picked up some goodies.

Peter's home is on Windmill Hill, just before reaching Enfield, a rural community about eight miles out from White River Junction. As I turned in the drive, I gasped. I had to stop and take it all in. Two brick pillars, with three globe lights of graduating sizes on the top, stood on either side of the entrance. Various species of maple trees lined both sides of the drive, the leaves moving lazily, casting soft shadows on the ground. But it was the pond that took my breath away! Beside the driveway, in front of the house, several ducks were playing in the spray from a tall fountain set in the middle of a big pond. After gazing for a few moments, I came back to earth. *Wow! I can't sit here basking in this beauty all day.* When I pulled in, Peter came out to meet me, his face aglow.

"It's so nice to see you, Maggie."

"You too, Peter." I was thrilled at the sincerity in

his voice. "You didn't tell me that you live in a park. Goodness, I may not know how to act here," I exclaimed, admiring the landscape.

"Thank you," he replied, blushing at my flattery. "I suppose it depends on which set of eyes you're looking through. For a while, I couldn't see anything but what I didn't have. I don't seem to feel like that anymore. Just a twinge now and then. You're good medicine, I think, Maggie, doll."

My heart fluttered at the affection I heard in his voice. "You do have quite the green thumb, don't you," I said, taking in the blue junipers by the front door, several shrubs and a couple flower beds, with various flowers in different stages of bloom, much like my own. "And I love the pond and the fountain!" I could visualize sitting out there with my morning coffee, watching the ducks frolicking. I'm sure a lot of this was Sandi's vision, but he'd done a good job keeping it up.

"Well, they certainly don't compare to yours, but then most people don't get that carried away, do they?" he said, giving me a jab in the ribs. "I suppose they could use some TLC, but I seem to have been preoccupied lately, eh?"

"Oh, that happens sometimes," I said, returning his mischievous grin.

"Well, let's go inside. I have the water boiled. Would you like tea or coffee?"

"Well, actually, I'll just have hot water. I've already had my morning coffee so hot water is good. I brought us a snack. I thought you might not have had time to bake a pie so I stopped and got something." I hoped he wouldn't be offended.

Although it was warm outside, the inside was cool. The blinds were drawn and I couldn't help but think of Mom. She'd always kept it as dark as possible in warmer weather. We either couldn't afford blinds or else we were so far down the social ladder that blinds weren't included, so Mom just found something to hang up over the windows, usually a blanket. It did the job, but I had never got into that. I'd much rather have the light, and besides, I like being able to look out at my gardens.

At night, though, I like dim lights and I don't even close my curtains, now that Amos is gone. I joked to a friend about it. "When you close them, there always seems to be a stubborn crack at the top and you just know there's an eye looking in there." So I leave them open and I feel better.

Looking closer, I couldn't believe my eyes. The kitchen curtains had been tied in knots about halfway up, letting the breeze flow through when the window was open. Sam had done that in the bedroom, but he'd known better than to try it in the kitchen. *Maybe Peter hadn't got away with that before, either.* Still, it warmed my heart.

Peter made himself a cup of tea and poured me some hot water and we sat in front of the window in two rocking chairs facing each other, with a small rectangular table between them. The table looked like it might have been a school project. With the blinds drawn, I could only picture the fountain and the ducks swimming around, yakking at each other. *It would be a lovely view, if one could see it.*

I tore open the goody bag and got a couple of napkins from the counter. I got four actually, because I always need two. One just doesn't do it. Luke used to tell me I didn't know how to eat.

"This is good," Peter said, biting into an orange cranberry muffin. "I couldn't have made any better myself. I'm glad you thought of bringing something."

"These pecan danishes are sinfully good," I said, taking a bite. "Mmm...I love them. They say that sin feels awfully good, with abominable after effects. What do you think?" I asked, swallowing a bite.

"Oh, I don't know," he snorted, shaking his head. "It could be true. I haven't been on real good speaking terms with the proprietor there."

We'd been chatting for an hour when Peter invited me to take a stroll out to see his garden. He had all the usual stuff besides some rhubarb and asparagus. Everything was marked by putting the seed envelopes on a stick like Dad used to do. Two boards, nailed together in the shape of a cross, with aluminium plates tied on to rattle in the breeze, made an excellent scarecrow.

"Looks nice, Peter. You keep it so clean. Reminds me of when we were kids. It was our job, mine, Olivia's, and Rose's, to weed the garden and Dad's orders were that he didn't want to find a weed, not one. We worked our little hearts out pulling even the tiniest of the critters. I'm sure he didn't mean those three quarters of an inch high. No wonder he thought we were such great little workers! I must say, I like them that way, but I'd never have a minute outside my garden if I tried to keep them all like that."

"I enjoy it," he said. "I give any extra to the kids. I don't bother preserving or freezing anything, but I do like the fresh vegetables. Another week and I should have my second bunch of radishes. I plant the red ones early, and three weeks later, I plant some sweet white ones."

We sat in the lawn chairs in the shade of one of the maple trees, enjoying the peacefulness of the merry little breezes blowing softly through the leaves. Jolly round red Mr. Sun couldn't quite reach us through the thick canopy overhead.

I didn't want to leave, but it really was time to go. Peter took my hand as we walked towards my car. "I hate to see you go," he said, loneliness creeping into his voice. "When I go back in the house, it'll seem empty. When you're around, everything looks a little brighter, Maggie."

I turned to face him, making sure he saw my sincerity. "That's exactly how I feel when you leave, Peter. It's one of those bittersweet things, but when I'm with you, the world feels right again." Looking into his face, I saw my happiness and joy reflected there. I saw living again, really living.

The sound of a car driving in brought me back to the present. "That's Judah," Peter exclaimed. We hurried over to his car as he rolled the window down.

"How've you been, old man?" Judah said, his face lighting up at the sight of his friend. "You're so busy these days, I haven't seen much of you."

"Well, I have been a little busy. When I do have some spare time, I guess Maggie and I...Oh, I'm sorry, Judah. This is Maggie LaHaye." Looking at me, he nodded, "My friend, Judah, I was telling you about, Maggie."

"It's lovely to meet you, Judah. Peter's told me what good friends you are. Not that I think it'd be hard to be a friend to Peter," I joked, glancing at Peter.

"You turkey," Peter said, putting his arm around my waist. "What am I going to do with her, Judah?"

Judah raised his eyebrow with an amused 'Do you need to ask me?' look. "I'll let you figure that one out, Peter."

Looking at me, he said "It is nice to meet you, Maggie. I must say that I was curious as to what woman would be able to turn Peter's head. You must be blessed with some special charms, I'd say. I can see he's happy, though," he said, obviously delighted for his friend.

"Oh I am, Judah," Peter agreed. "More than I ever thought I could be," the affection in his voice warming my heart as a smile flashed across his face and he gave me a quick wink. Turning back to Judah he said, "I think I even surprised myself."

Judah nodded, looking us over, a soft smile playing about his mouth. "Nice surprise," he grinned, putting the car in reverse. "We'll have you over sometime soon. I saw you outside and just wanted to say 'hey.'"

Chapter 9

Supper at Luke's

WE WERE INVITED TO LUKE AND KATE'S for supper. Arriving a little early, we found Nicholas and his friend Jacob in the garage working on Nick's ATV. Nick, fifteen, is a younger version of Luke, but with a lot more hair, golden brown and long in the front, falling nicely to his eyebrows. Jacob is fifteen, slim with dark hair cut short on the sides while the top is covered with a mass of curls falling on his forehead.

Peter asked Nick about what he was doing, nodding his head as Nick explained about the valve job they were undertaking, Peter not mentioning that he's a mechanic. Nick has learned a lot, following his dad's directions, being Luke's hands in many ways, since his accident.

Kate, a slim woman with short brown hair and a pleasant smile, met us at the door, vibrant as always. "Hello, hello. It's lovely to meet you, Peter," she greeted him, in her English accent. "I've heard a bit about you, you know."

I flushed and Peter said, "Pleased to meet you, too, Kate," as he helped me with my jacket. I knew his eyes were sparkling, revelling in the banter. "I've heard what a wonderful daughter-in-law you are. I hope what you've heard about me is half as complimentary."

"Oh, I won't tell tales, Peter," she said, catching my eye.

"We're even now," Peter whispered, putting his hand on my cheek.

Kate's son, Liam, from a previous relationship, is also fifteen, with dark curly hair. He was coming from his room, just in time for introductions.

Kate had made her famous carrot soup and pork tenderloin and her English version of lemon pie, which she knows I love. "This is delicious, Kate," Peter said, tasting the carrot soup. She beamed.

Luke asked Peter about his work. Although Peter is a mechanic and welder by trade, he has been a truck driver most of his life. He'd started out with a pulp truck and one year, when the logging industry was slow, he got a gravel truck and hauled gravel when he wasn't hauling pulp. He also has a straight truck and an eighteen-wheeler. He hauls mostly produce and frozen foods from wholesalers to their distribution centers.

He's kept all of his trucks. He says they're paid for and he might as well keep them and he'll always be able to find work of one sort or another. His training as a mechanic has come in handy, saving him considerable money over the years.

As we were finishing dessert, Sebastian came in.

At nineteen, he's over six feet tall, very slim, and I'm pleased to see that his hair is its natural medium blond. When it's longer, it curls, nice soft curls. When it's short, he likes it jelled in the new style, slicked up in the front. He went through a phase where he was experimenting with black hair, black/blue and purplish/black. I like the blond much better. Both my grandsons have long curly eyelashes that most girls would die for and I kind of envy.

"I had to come by and see Nan's new friend that I've been hearing so much about," Sebastian said.

Peter looked at me, his eyes crinkling. We weren't even anymore and he loved it.

Sebastian looked at Peter. "You have to be Peter. I'm Sebastian. Nan will probably tell you my name is Jonathan and that's true, but I think Sebastian suits me better, at least for now. If you forget, I answer to either. I'm very pleased to meet you," he said, extending his hand. I was proud of how comfortable he seemed, not waiting for someone else to introduce him.

Peter stood and shook his hand. "It's lovely to meet you, Sebastian. I think that's a nice name and it seems to suit you just fine."

As Peter was finishing his pie, he looked at Luke. "It looks like you've got a good cook, Luke. That's always a bonus for us men, eh? I mean a fellow might find the nicest woman who couldn't cook worth beans. That would be a hard spot to be in. So if you get both, well, you're pretty fortunate, by my books," he said, casting a sly glance in my direction.

A smug little feeling crept over me. *Sam and Amos sure liked my cooking.*

While Kate and I cleared the table, the men wandered into the living room, chatting easily. Peter's charm was irresistible and it was obvious that he thought I was the cat's pyjamas. I knew my family was happy for me.

I overheard Luke say, "My mom's pretty special, isn't she, Peter? I can see you think a lot of her."

I was picking up the silverware from the table and couldn't resist looking up. Peter looked over at me while choosing his words. Our eyes met and I smiled. "Yes, I do, Luke," he agreed, his voice warm. "Actually, I think she's a pretty rare jewel. But don't tell her I said so," he added, confidentially. "I rather like hanging out with her and we seem to have a lot of fun for a couple of old grandparents."

"I haven't seen her so happy in a long time," Luke said, a look of relief flooding his face.

"We'll have to see what we can do to see more of that, then," Peter said, obviously flattered by the compliment.

Peter asked Nicholas more about his ATV. "I have lots of room in my garage. You could bring it out and I might even give you a hand with it, that is, if your dad doesn't mind."

Looking at Nick, Luke said, "It's okay with me. Sure, I'll take it out for him if he wants to do that."

"I guess," Nick said, shrugging his shoulders. They decided they'd take it out on Monday. I was pleased with Peter offering to help. Luke's garage is small and with all his tools stored in there, space is limited. Peter has a big garage for his trucks, so it did make sense.

Before we knew it, ten o'clock had rolled around. "I'd best be getting this lady home," Peter said. Luke lives in Windsor, about forty minutes from my place and then Peter would have to drive back. He lived another half hour past Luke's.

After hugs and good-byes, we made our way out to the truck. Kate later told me that as Luke looked out the window, the sight of Peter putting his arm around his mother's shoulder filled him with emotion. "I'm so happy for Mom," he said, his voice catching, as he reached up for her to take his hand. "I hope Peter is what he seems to be."

Sebastian called the following day. "You have to hang on to that fellow, Nan," he said. "He's a keeper." Chuckling, I said he wouldn't be getting away if I had anything to say about it!

Chapter 10

Maggie Blushes

I GUESS I INHERITED DAD'S PLEASURE in making silly rhymes, but I think I'm even sillier than he is. He seems to have tamed down some now in his old age.

Sometimes I pick up one of my dogs and dance around with him or her, singing my own version of Patti Page's "How Much Is That Doggie In The Window?"

> How much is that doggie in the window
> The one with the waggily tail
> I'd like to have that doggie in the window
> I do hope that doggie's for sale
>
> I don't want a mansion or a caddie
> I don't want a shepherd or pug
> I just want that little Maltese Poodle
> I just want my Cinnamon to love
>
> or
>
> I just want that little old Shih Tzu
> I just want my Cookie to love

or

I just want that little old Yorkie
I just want my Kiwi to love

Or sometimes it's "My Darling Clementine," just changing Clementine to the dog's name and making the rest of it rhyme. That's what I was singing today with Kiwi.

Oh my darling, Oh my darling
Oh my darling Kiwi babe
You're the sweetest little Yorkie
And I am oh so glad you came.

I had put Kiwi down and was picking Cinnamon up when I heard someone saying, "Are you okay, Maggie?"

Who could that be? I hurriedly put the dog down, turning to check myself in the mirror. Probably my hair was flying every which way. *Oh, it's Peter.* He was standing in the living-room doorway, an amused look on his face.

"Oh, Peter, it's you. How are you doing?" I said, blushing a little at being caught in my childish play.

"Oh, I'm okay," he replied, raising his eyebrows. "But are you? Maybe it's a good thing I asked if I could come calling before I heard that serenade."

O-o-o-h-h, sounds like he's up for some fun.

"Oh now, let's not get jealous, Peter." I walked over to him, putting one arm around his waist and the other hand on his shoulder, pulling him into the room as I started singing and dancing, tossing his hat on the couch.

Oh my darling, Oh my darling

Oh my darling Peter dear

You're the sweetest man I've seen around

And I am oh so glad you're here.

I looked up at him, smiling my shameless pleasure.

"I can't dance. I'll probably step on your feet," he chuckled softly.

I paid no attention and when I finished, I said "Goodness, I can't dance properly either, Peter. I just have fun dancing to my own beat." I laid my head on his shoulder as we continued to dance slowly, if you could call it dancing, while I softly hummed "It's Such A Pretty World."

When we stopped, I didn't move away but looked up and, in mock seriousness, asked, "Peter, are you going to leave me because I'm a little silly?"

His eyes were as soft as velvet as he pulled me to him. "I wouldn't dream of it, Maggie. I admire a person who's not afraid to be who they really are." With his chin resting on the top of my head, he said, "I think I could get used to dancing to your beat."

My heart quickened. *I could even adjust my beat a little, if it would help.*

After a moment, I reluctantly stepped back from his light embrace. "I wasn't expecting you today. Are you taking a load somewhere?"

"No, I had the afternoon off and wondered if you'd like to go for a drive. We could go see some of the falls in Mass and maybe get an ice cream."

"Oh, I'd love that. Just give me a minute." I quickly changed my skirt and fixed my hair. "Okay, all set!" I said, as I sashayed into the room.

"Are you bringing our pals?" Peter asked.

"Well, since we might be getting ice cream, I think not. They'd just want to eat mine," I said, nonchalantly.

Looking surprised, he said, "You wouldn't let them, would you?"

"I just said they'd want to. Let's leave it at that," I answered, leaving him to wonder.

He had his car today, a white Buick with a red top. Instead of going around to the passenger side, he opened his door and stood back. "You can get in here, if you like."

I slid under the steering wheel, smelling the sweet scent of the lavender pomander hanging from the mirror. I was getting used to the smell since Peter had one in every vehicle I'd been in. I sat, not in the middle, but about halfway between the middle and the passenger door, turning towards him and making myself comfortable.

"Nice car, Peter. You must like white." All the trucks I'd seen were white with red lettering, but I was surprised that his car was white, too.

"I guess the first vehicle I bought was a red and white half-ton and I liked it. My first pulp truck was tan, but when I bought the gravel truck, it was white. So the next pulp truck, I ordered white. And it went from there. I still have the half-ton. It's in the garage. I've kept it up, but I've left it red and white."

"I hope you're not as bad as my brother-in-law, Brian. He's a real fanatic about his vehicles. They all have to be Fords or they don't sit in his driveway. And they all have to be parked a certain way, probably within an inch of the space he has allotted."

Changing the subject, I asked, "Did you hear about the woman whose cat liked ice cream? The cat was in her basket in the back seat and the mistress kept reaching back for Mittens to get a lick. When they arrived wherever they were going, she was shocked to see that Mittens was looking towards the back. She said it was all she could do to keep from upchucking, realizing she'd been sharing her ice cream with the cat's rear end."

"Are you serious?" he asked, looking mortified.

"That's the way I heard it."

"And have you ever noticed," I went on, "how, at least some dogs' tongues are coated with slime?" He looked at me like the word 'nutcase' might be trying to force its way into his thoughts. "Yeah, Cookie's is like that, or at least his is worse than the others. I don't notice Cinnamon's and Kiwi's being that bad. So I think I shouldn't let them eat my ice cream. Don't you agree?" I asked, trying to keep an innocent expression on my face.

"I don't know whether to believe you or not," he said, chuckling. "I think you're pulling my leg."

I snickered, not able to conceal my mischief, but

decided I'd better drop the foolishness.

"So Peter, tell me one of your deep dark secrets. You must have one or two."

"I'll have to think," he said. "I'll let you know when I remember something."

We drove in silence for a while and when Peter started singing "What A Friend We Have In Jesus," I joined him. *He's heard me singing my silly songs, so I might as well sing along with him. And I'm probably no more off-key than he.*

After a little while of serenading each other and some rather interesting harmonizing, Peter said, "Well, this isn't a 'dark' secret, but it's just one of my finicky things. We all must have a couple of those, I suppose. I can't wait to find out what yours is. I'm sure it won't be anything that the rest of us would stress over!"

"I'd better smarten up!" I said, quickly. "I think maybe you're beginning to wonder if I might be a little off my rocker." I turned and looked out the window, feigning concern, but couldn't help bursting into laughter.

"I...I don't think you're off your rocker, but you sure are unique," he said, a smile tugging at the corners of his mouth. "I'll admit though that it's been a long time since I've had so much fun." He couldn't keep the soft laughter from his voice. Looking at me, he chuckled, "Maybe I'm catching it too.

"I forgot what we were talking about," he said. "Oh, yes. Dishes in the sink all the time. Yeah, that's what drives me crazy! It seemed that Mom always had dirty dishes in the sink, and I thought, *when I get a place of my own, I think I'll put up a fuss if my wife does that.*"

"Oh ye-e-s," I said, my eyes dancing with glee. "And did you help her keep the dishes out of the sink or did you just fill it up?"

"I did when she let me."

"Let you? What do you mean, 'let you'?" I asked, feigning surprise. "I wouldn't be turning down the help of a handsome man. I might just keep the sink full so he'd have to help me," I said, barely able to keep my face straight.

"You're a torment, Maggie. You want to be careful, a fellow might take you serious and get too big for his britches."

"Really? Well, the fellow I had in mind is much too nice for that. If he wasn't, his seams might have burst long ago. Everyone seems to love him, but he's not struck on himself, or at least he doesn't show it. But I'll keep that in mind. I wouldn't want to be responsible for anything like that.

"On a more serious note," I asked, "how did you make out with Nick's ATV?"

"We got it pretty well done. They're coming out again on the weekend and we should be able to get it finished. He's a nice boy, Maggie. Very polite. I'm surprised at what he knows about mechanics."

"Yes, I guess I am, too. I sure love it when he can do my repair work. I usually give him a few bucks, although he doesn't expect it. He's comical though. He says when he grows up he doesn't want to have to work hard but wants lots of money so he can pay someone else to do the things he doesn't want to do. I tell him he'd best get to university then," I laughed.

"Yes, that's probably good advice," Peter said.

We decided to get a sundae while making up our minds on which falls we'd visit. We'd just got seated when Sherry came in. When she got her banana split, I called to her to come and join us.

"Peter," she said, "I don't know what your secret is, but my sister looks ten years younger since she's been hanging out with you."

"Oh, I don't have any special secret, but we won't tell her that. She's pretty good company, too, you know."

After hanging out with Sherry for a while, we drove to the Slatestone Brook Falls. They make a lovely backdrop, surrounded by sea-green moss while fanning and dropping several times over the huge boulders.

The falls is situated between two houses, one only thirty feet away. It must be a soothing treat listening to the gurgling water spilling over the rocks, lulling one's senses into total relaxation before dropping off to sleep each night. Then, maybe the residents get used to the sound and don't even hear it.

We were able to walk right up to the Gunbrook Falls, after scrambling down the rather steep trail. Some folks were walking out to have their picture taken, standing on top of one of the fifteen or twenty foot plunges. That wasn't for me! Parents were enjoying watching their children playing in the chilly but gentle waters at the base. We took lots of pictures with our phones, giggling like teenagers.

What a lovely afternoon! As we drove back, the sun was shining brightly. The river, as smooth as glass, cast a clear reflection of the trees on the opposite bank. "You're awfully quiet," Peter commented. "Tired?"

"Oh...I was just admiring the river. I love it. It's so peaceful and relaxing. Some things improve with age, don't you think?"

"Never thought much about it," he said.

"When I was growing up, it was just the river, nothing special. But after I'd been away, when I came back, it looked more beautiful than I remembered it. And it started talking to me. It'd say things like, 'Don't let yourself get all worked up. Just relax. Enjoy life. See how easily I flow. The quieter I am, the less I have to work. I've even heard you say that I'm soothing when I'm quiet.' Yeah, the river has taught me a few things about life," I said, thoughtfully.

"I've thought about that a lot. My theory is that common sense is a good trade-off for some of the down sides of aging."

"Are you talking in circles, Maggie?"

"Circles?" I asked innocently, still looking at the river. "I don't see any circles, do you? I just see curves and bends. It looks pretty clear to me. No, I don't see any circles." I turned, smiling at him, and he couldn't help but grin.

Changing the subject, I asked "You know what one of my finicky things is? The white thing in an egg. I have to take that out. Not many people know how to get it out of a boiled egg, but I've figured that out, too.

"Another thing that bothers me is having to touch a chair in a restaurant. Or the salt and pepper shakers. I'm glad someone came up with the idea of hand sanitizer."

"So that's why you're always using that stuff. Interesting. Actually, I never thought of that before. I guess it's true, but I'm not sure I want to go there. I'll leave that one to you," he said, with a snort.

"I suppose not," I said. "I'm not as bad as my aunt, though. At eighty, when she used a public restroom, she'd reach up with her foot and flush the toilet so she didn't have to touch the handle with her hands. I thought I'd die laughing when she told me that. She hadn't learned to take the first few blocks of tissue off and throw them away, though. I had to teach her that. But no, we certainly don't need to add any more stress to our lives."

The dogs were overjoyed to see us when we returned.

Peter decided he had time for a coffee, so while I went to make it, he sat down on the sofa, talking to the dogs. Cinnamon had jumped on his lap and Miss Kiwi sat on the cushion on the floor, whining. Cookie surveyed the situation and decided he'd just sit at Peter's feet for the time being.

RHONDA CRONKHITE

The coffee was soon ready and we chatted easily, sipping the hot liquid and enjoying the date bread I'd defrosted.

The time flew by quickly, as always, and I was dreading to see Peter leave. I thought about asking him to stay for supper, but I didn't want to appear too eager. He did seem to enjoy my company, though, so I decided to risk it.

"I'm getting a little hungry, Peter, I think I'll make a chicken salad sandwich. Would you like one?"

He hesitated for just a second. "Well, if it's not too much trouble, I guess I could find room for one," he said.

"My pleasure," I said, getting the chicken from the fridge.

"Do you mind if I put some music on?" he asked.

"Be my guest. I love music. We grew up on it," I called over my shoulder. "We listened to a lot of the Phillips Brothers and the Louvin Brothers. We often had records going day and night, literally. Whoever got up in the night often flipped the stack over and we had a few more hours of enjoyment. Well, most of it was enjoyment. There were some that I dreaded coming on in the daylight, let alone in the middle of the night. I remember "A Pretty Wreath For Mother's Grave," or "The Wreck On The Highway," or "Will The Circle Be Unbroken." Those songs made me nervous. They felt like bad omens to me."

"Really?" he asked. "We never had much music playing at home, but I like it now. I've never heard about Mother's Grave or The Wreck on the Highway. I suppose they aren't happy songs."

"Yeah," I said, "we did". "It's interesting though, after you've lost someone, some of those songs are comforting. Well, not "The Wreck On The Highway," or "The Dying Drunkard's Plea, either." That was another one I dreaded...those aren't, but the other ones are nice." I thought about how not only had the songs made me nervous, but everything about death had scared me. Just driving by the graveyard sent chills up and down my spine. Now I can go there with my coffee and sit down and have a nice visit. *What's there to be scared of?*

Coming back to the present, I said, "Sam was always singing "Where The Roses Never Fade" and "I Won't Have To Cross Jordan Alone." It made me uneasy. I had them sung at his funeral, and now I love them. That's another word I don't like: 'funeral'. It just sounds so...dead.

"I didn't have a funeral for Amos."

Glancing up, I saw his questioning look.

"Oh, I had a service. It just wasn't a funeral service. One of those in a lifetime is enough. Well, more than enough. So we had a 'Celebration of Life'. It is whatever you call it, right?

"I wouldn't have thought about that with Sam, but then, that was a funeral service. I was twenty years old and I hadn't had him long enough to celebrate enough. He was snatched away and I couldn't think of anything positive right then. It was a funeral alright."

The Unexpected Love

We decided to sit on the front deck and enjoy watching the river slipping lazily by. Savouring the fresh sandwich, topped with lettuce, pickles and tomatoes, I picked up where I'd left off. "I wouldn't say I was ever a negative person but when you've just met the man of your dreams… just starting your life together…and all of a sudden, he's snatched away…it's quite a shock.

"I don't remember how long it was before I felt like life was worth living again. It's just an awful time to remember. But, goodness, how'd I get on that? I'm sorry for rambling on, Peter."

As I set my drink down, he put his hand over mine. When I looked up, his eyes were gentle with understanding. "It's all right, Maggie. There's nothing to be sorry about. That's part of your life. It's a part of who you are today and I don't see anything wrong with that. That's just the way it is." I nodded.

I didn't say it, but even now there was a fleeting vision of Sam's head above the water as he struggled to...to what? To live? To come home with us? I've thought about that speck of a second when he knew he wasn't going to make it, knew he was going down, seeing us on the shore but not able to say anything.

When we finished eating, Peter asked if I'd like to go for a walk. We could check out the gardens or we could walk down and see my Aunt Josie.

"Yes, let's do that. I don't go to see her nearly enough. I'm really quite a homebody."

Aunt Josie was delighted to see us and offered us a cup of coffee. Peter had one, but I really didn't have room for anything.

Peter can talk to people so easily, like he's always known them. We chatted for a half hour and decided it was time to get back. We were almost there when I shouted, "Race you to the mailbox! One…two…three." Peter looked surprised but was soon even with me. He sprinted ahead and reached the driveway a couple seconds ahead of me, skidding to a stop and turning around just in time to catch me as I came in second...just about as winded as he was.

"You're pretty good, Peter. You're only the second fellow who has ever beat me in a race, you know."

"Yeah? Tell me another one," guffawed.

"It's the truth. I think Luke won when he was a teenager, and probably the only reason was that his legs were so long," I laughed.

I remembered the night Sam had challenged me to race to the house. I saw that I was going to win and slackened my pace just enough to let him finish first. I think he realized it and we never raced again. I wouldn't be so silly today. I should have won and told him he couldn't be the best at everything…he was still the sweetest and most handsome man around. But Peter had beat me fair and square.

Heading up the drive, Peter asked, "Where did you get the idea for your circles over there? I've never seen anything quite like that."

"Oh, I haven't either," I said. "That's just another one of the creations I dreamed up. Let's take a walk over." I have two large cement circles, one standing up inside the other, and a smaller one standing up inside that one, at an angle. Wisteria on either side was growing up around the top, with tendrils hanging over the front. I'd planted my roses around it, the yellow climbing one, Mom's pink bush, and her little rose I'd stunted when I stepped on it the night she died. We passed the vegetable garden and the row of lilac bushes, now wilted and brown. The larger Japanese one at the end would soon be boasting its' large creamy blossoms, the buds about ready to burst open.

There was my garden art, for that's what I call my circle combination, sitting proudly between the fruit and nut orchards. I'd planted several different ground covers around the base in an effort to keep the weeding to a minimum. The strawberries and raspberries were just beyond, the strawberries just starting to ripen.

When Dad lived here, he gave me several locust trees that I'd transplanted in White River Junction, where we were living at the time. When we bought this place, I'd brought one back. Now, it's planted on the property line above the orchards. I try to keep it pruned back so it won't get so massive and lose its beauty. I think the fifty-foot ones are ugly and bear no resemblance to the spectacular young ones, and I'm not going to let mine be boss. I get pretty vicious with the pruning and plan to keep them looking young for as long as I can. A low rock wall around the tree borders the gaillardia growing beneath it.

I love locust trees; they stir such fond memories of

when we were kids, playing under the smaller ones, making tents with Mom's blankets. That's why I call my place Locust Lane. I'd found some little ones sprouting across the road and had planted three of them at the beginning of the driveway. Only one lived, but it's still Locust Lane.

We walked up past the raspberries and over to the large round bed at the back, bordered with dianthus and Lombardy poplars. Several White Birch and a massive Golden Ninebark surround the stove room, off to the side.

After one of my dreaming sessions, Amos had built a little room out of old bricks. The walls are only seven feet high, with the bricks going up four feet with the remaining three feet screened in. Dad had given me a glass door that I'd been hanging on to, so I'd painted it the colour of the house trim.

We'd put Dad's old airtight stove in the back corner, painting it with a heat and weather resistant black paint. We covered it up in the winter to protect it. A pile of wood sat beside it, ready for a chilly evening when two old geezers wanted to sit in the little porch rocking chairs. Or they might just need one of the chairs.

We walked past the fire pit that had materialized after we tore down the two-story shop and garage Dad had enjoyed countless hours building. He hadn't put a footing under it and the floor had rotted out. It had been a great source of enjoyment to him, filling his long days. Then we were back at the greenhouse so we sat in the picnic room for a few minutes.

All of these trees and shrubs had given my brother-in-law, Brian, much stress; he had helped Dad with the mowing and plowing when he and Mom were still living here. I thought it was all worth the extra trouble, even if I did have to do it alone now.

Amos had never complained when I decided I needed some help with another bed, or planting more trees. I guess he'd learned that it was just part of life with me and he might as well get in the spirit of it. I think he enjoyed seeing me act like a kid with a new toy and it kept him busy between my visits. He knew there was no stopping my dreaming, and he enjoyed making at least some of them come true.

I've always found the gardens restful. I'd take my coffee out in the morning and sit for a few minutes in one of the chairs by the picnic room while Samson, the wooden bear I'd won at the garden center, stood guard at the corner of the greenhouse.

After several sips, I'd have enough energy to meander through it all and see what had changed since yesterday. It truly is my therapy and I always reason that every addition decreases the mowing a little, even if it does take longer. Brian can have his four-acre lot with five trees if he wants. What he saw as work, I see as pleasure. Of course, I hadn't had all this when he was helping, or he'd probably have had a heart attack or a stroke from the stress it would have given him. From my perspective, though, it was a stress reliever that probably saved me from having one.

It really was time for Peter to head home and my

heart wasn't fluttering or purring. It suddenly felt like I had a heavy weight in my chest with an invisible thread connected to my mouth, making me look rather glum, I'm sure. I was already anticipating the empty feeling I knew would be there when he was gone.

It was quickly becoming more difficult for Peter to leave and even harder for me to see him go.

Chapter 11

Lonesome

PETER HAD TO MAKE A LONG HAUL, taking a load of potatoes to Florida and bringing back some fruit. He'd have to wait a couple of days for the fruit order, so he'd be gone over a week. We were both dreading it.

We talked on the phone every evening, but it was still lonely. Peter always stopped by if he was in the area so we usually saw each other every few days.

One evening he said, "You haven't had any fellows in checking to see if you need any help, have you, Maggie?"

"You mean someone who just realized he should be helping the widows?" I asked, chuckling. "As a matter of fact, Tommy Woods did come by the other day. He saw me in the garden and stopped to chat. I guess he did ask if I needed any help, but I told him I was pretty well looked after."

"Well, I guess I can't blame the fellow for having good taste, can I?" Peter chuckled.

"About as much as I can blame those waitresses down there for the way I know they're looking at you.

I can hear them saying, 'Hey, d'you see that - they'd probably call you a hunk or something, but I don't talk like that - that handsome fellow who just came in? He's stunning! And I don't see a ring either. I'll have to keep my eye on him.' So I guess I can't blame them for having good eye sight either, can I?" I said, returning his good natured teasing.

I've never considered myself to be a jealous woman, but I do have boundaries. Being young and immature, I'd had no idea how to communicate my feelings when someone had flirted with Sam on a couple of occasions.

There was one time when Sam was being a brat himself and smiling at the girl. Our friend, Ken, was with us, with one sitting on either side of me so I suppose she thought I was with Ken. She'd have certainly never guessed I was the wife of this handsome dude, with me smiling, too. But when I thought it had gone too far, I got up and walked out. It wasn't long before Sam and Ken came out acting like two scared sheep. Today, I'd have just whispered, "Sam, you're going to get yourself in trouble." It wasn't that I didn't trust him but it made me look rather stupid, and I didn't like that.

So I meant it when I joked about the girls looking at Peter. They'd have to be blind not to notice his charming looks and character, but I certainly wasn't jealous. I didn't see any need to be.

"Okay, that's enough now. I get the picture," Peter said. "But I can't wait to get home. Would you like to go to dinner when I get back?"

"I could do that. I'm going to Luke's in the afternoon, so I could meet you afterwards."

"Well, better yet, if you're coming up, why don't I make supper for you? I've been wanting to make some chili. Do you like chili?"

"I love chili. Would you like me to bring some biscuits? Biscuits are great with chili."

"Why don't you just make them when you get there and then we can have them warm? Besides, that would mean you'd have to come a little earlier, right? We can sit around afterwards and listen to some music, or whatever you'd like to do."

"I'll be there. What time?....oh never mind. I'll come early," I said, my heart feeling all warm and fuzzy.

Chapter 12

A Letter

I WAS SURPRISED WHEN I CHECKED the mail the next day and there was a letter from Peter. It was a card with pink and white lily of the valley, on a dark pink background. It read, "Missing You" and inside he'd written, "It's very lonely down here so thought I'd send you a note.

"I've been missing you a lot. You're good medicine when you're around, Maggie my doll, but the withdrawal symptoms are pretty tough.

"I'm looking forward to seeing you when I get back.

"Lovingly, Peter."

I walked back to the house with a smug smile and a light heart.

Chapter 13

Reflecting

BEFORE GOING TO PETER'S ON SATURDAY, I stopped to visit with Luke and Kate for a while. Luke asked how Peter and I were doing.

"We're doing fine. Peter's a nice man."

"You must be getting rather serious. You seem to be together a lot."

"Well...I'm not sure how to answer that. I like Peter a lot. I could be serious about him, but I've never been one to chase a man or put ideas in his head that he can't think of on his own. He's never had a girlfriend since Sandi's been gone so I do feel pretty special to be his friend."

"Well, I think he's a good man, Mom. I hope it works out for you. And it's nice to see you so happy."

"Thank you sweetheart. I am happy. I'm going out to Peter's this afternoon. He's making chili for supper and I'm making biscuits."

Luke rolled his eyes. "Pretty serious, if you ask me, Mom."

Peter must have heard me drive in. He came out to

meet me, all smiles. "It's so nice to see you, Maggie. I've missed you dreadfully," he said, hugging me tight for a moment.

My heart was dancing and I wondered if his was, too. "Me too," I sighed. "It was a long two weeks."

The aroma of the simmering chili reminded me that I was getting hungry. Peter had the table set and some classical music playing softly in the background.

"I opened the blinds today," he said. "I didn't realize how dark it was in here until after you left the other day. I thought you might like them better open."

"Oh, well, I don't close mine but everyone's different." All of a sudden, I realized I didn't give a hoot which way the blinds were. "That's fine if you like them closed. When you're around, Peter, you're light enough. At least, that's how it looks through my glasses."

"Well, I think I like your glasses," he chuckled. "Keep wearing them."

I washed my hands and turned the oven on and asked where I'd find the cooking ingredients and utensils. Peter got everything out and I got busy sifting and measuring. Sometimes I sift my dry ingredients three times. I'd do that today; I wanted them to be perfect.

Taking extra time, putting ice in the milk and beating the egg up really well paid off because they raised beautifully. I always cut my biscuits at least an inch thick to start with, so their hike isn't quite so long. They were as light as a feather, and perfectly golden.

The chili was superb, not too hot, just the way I like it. Well, I would have added a little more sugar, but it was delicious.

The dining room is on the front of the house so we watched the ducks in the pond and the traffic going by while we ate. As we were finishing, a car drove in.

"Sounds like you have company, Peter. Were you expecting someone?"

"It's probably Zeke. When I told them you were coming for supper, Ruby wanted to make a pie. She asked what your favourite is and I told her I thought either lemon meringue or graham cracker. Was I right?"

"That's exactly my two favourites. I actually like all cream pies. The only pies I don't eat are raisin and mincemeat. I'm told that I'm missing something, but I'm perfectly okay with that," I said, putting my hand up to emphasize my certainty in the matter.

Zeke opened the door, calling "Delivery Service. Did you order a pie? I was told to bring it to house number 355."

"Come on in, Zeke," his dad called. "I didn't really order it. But that wife of yours is so sweet, she wanted to make it for Maggie. So what could I say?"

"Well, that looks super delicious," I said, "and pie is one of my weaknesses." It was almost four inches high, with fluffy thick meringue.

"Your Dad has some tea made, Zeke. Would you like to have a piece with us and a cup of tea?"

"I think she made us one, too," he said, "but I'd have a cup of tea."

"I'll get it," Peter said.

"Did you make those biscuits, Dad? I didn't know you could make biscuits," Zeke asked.

"No, a little elf made them. Would you like to try one?"

"I don't mind if I do," he said, and started to get up to get a saucer and a knife.

"Sit still," his dad said. "I'll get it for you."

"You be sure and give my thanks to Ruby for the pie. That was so sweet of her. You have a nice wife, Zeke."

"I do," he said. "I think she's sweeter than she was when we were first married. I can't imagine what it must be like to lose someone you love so much. I think I'd have a hard job staying sane."

"Humph," I retorted, a little too forcefully. "The alternative to staying sane isn't very pleasant." Softening my tone, I went on, "It's certainly not a position anyone wants to be in. One has to make the best of things, though, or end up being such a nuisance that no one wants you around," I finished, rolling my eyes in jest.

"You're probably right. I have a lot of respect for anyone who can manage to pull themselves together and make the most of a bad situation. Dad seems so much happier since you and he started hanging out together. It's nice to see him enjoying life again."

"It appears you've all been good to him, and he's

lucky to have children like that. In all honesty, I think it may be harder for men on some levels because usually the woman keeps things running smoothly in the house and a lot of men don't know anything about cooking or cleaning. But I guess we do have to adapt to our situation. There really isn't any other choice."

"I suppose you're right. I think Dad has done well. He's been strong."

"He's told me about you all having dinner together on Sunday and coming here on Sunday evening to spend time with him. And that you each have him for supper one night a week. I'd say he has quite a special family."

"Well, he's always been a good dad and we love having him around. I must say I was a little surprised when he told us he was seeing someone. But it's been good for him."

"Thank you, Zeke. I certainly enjoy his company."

He finished his biscuit. "I must be heading home. Ruby will have supper ready. That biscuit was delicious. It was nice seeing you again, Maggie, and enjoy your pie."

"That I will, Zeke. And don't forget to tell Ruby how much I appreciate it."

Peter went out with Zeke and I cleared up the dishes. I noticed there was a dishwasher, but since there weren't many, I'd do them by hand.

I put some country gospel music on, whistling softly along with it. I can still see my grandmother sitting in her rocking chair, legs apart and dress pulled down over her knees, whistling. She didn't sound much better than I do. Amos sometimes told me that I really couldn't whistle, but that didn't stop me from trying. When I'm driving, I often whistle along with the music or practise singing in my softer voice. I think I may have actually improved a little.

Whistling away as I rattled the dishes, I was surprised when I glanced up to see Peter standing at the corner of the fridge, an amused smirk on his face.

"You're one interesting character, Maggie. I suspect there's not another one like you."

"Let's hope not," I said, feeling my face flush. "Can you imagine there being two loons like this in the world? I wouldn't trade places with any sane person though; I'm quite happy being my own free spirit.

"Dad was always whistling tunes when we were young. It bugged me that I could never get the sound to come out right. He said 'Whistling girls and crowing men always come to some bad end.' I didn't see any crowing men so I didn't understand the problem. We were a little backwards, you know. I just learned recently that it's not 'crowing men' it's 'crowing hens.' We had our own vocabulary; we said 'culbert' for 'culvert' and 'crick' for 'creek' and fuller for fellow. And then Mom discovered 'lustoil', the greatest thing for taking pitch out of Dad's work pants. And beef 'burilli', we loved that. It never tasted quite the same when we discovered it was only beef ravioli. I do have to laugh when I catch myself reading like Mom.

RHONDA CRONKHITE

"The last few years, I decided I didn't care whether I was a pro whistler or not, I enjoy it." I lowered my voice confidentially, "I heard Kate one day coming up the stairs, whistling the most off-key tune, but it had a smile in it. It sounded an awful lot like the noise I make, and I decided right then and there, I'd enjoy my whistling and not worry about anyone else's opinion."

"You don't have to do those dishes, you know," Peter said. "I can do them after you leave."

"I want to do them. It's doesn't matter what we're doing, we can still talk and you can help me while we talk. Or if you don't want to talk, we can whistle."

When the dishes were finished, we went into the living room. Peter turned on some lamps and put some softer music on.

I sat on the sofa, curling one foot underneath myself, while Peter sat down facing me. "That was a nice supper, Peter. Thanks for inviting me."

"You're as welcome as the flowers in May, as my dad used to say."

We sat quietly, listening to the music for a few minutes. Breaking the silence, I said, "There's something I want to say, Peter. I just need to say it and I'll feel better."

He looked at me, furrowing his brow.

"I'm sure you've probably thought of this, too, but then, maybe it's different for women. I was thinking, while we were doing the dishes, about this having been Sandi's kitchen and here I am washing dishes with her husband.

"I know all the logical arguments, but I can't help wondering how she'd feel. Then, I wonder if when they get to the other side, they look back and see this old world and realize that they're in a much better place, and maybe that makes it different somehow."

"I know what you mean," he said, slowly nodding his head, sounding relieved.

"Sam and I were driving with his friend, Ken, one day when he told Ken he thought he'd cancel his life insurance policy because finances were a little tight. "He said, 'If something happened to me, Maggie would get married again, so she'd be okay.'

"Humph! How soon did he think I'd get married again? Of course, it really wasn't going to happen, either, right? 'Don't talk about stuff like that. You scare me.' I said. The thought of not having him and of marrying someone else was just too foreign. He was twenty but he could think that through. I wasn't thinking any such thing at all, let alone through.

"I've thought about it many times and wondered if it had been me who was taken, how I'd feel for him to have married someone else. There's a part of me that doesn't like that thought one bit, but then I wouldn't have wanted him to be sad and lonely, either.

"Here's what I really think. If something had happened to me, and after forty years, he still thought as much of me as I do of him, and had kept my memory alive for Luke as I have his, I think I'd be okay with that. But I wouldn't want him to be happier than he was with me, and I sure wouldn't want him to love her a speck more than he did me. Does that make sense?"

"I think it does," he said. "I've been thinking about those things, too, not quite sure how I felt about it."

"I respect that this was Sandi's home," I said, "and she took pride in it for her family. She just didn't know she wouldn't be here to look after you all. I guess I just want you to know that I'm aware of that."

He slid over beside me and put his arms around my shoulders. "I do know what you mean, and I'm glad you brought it up. Sandi and I were truly in love and I do still love her. I'll always treasure her memory. I'm glad to know that you still think that much of Sam and Amos. If you really love someone, you can't stop loving them, but we do have to live."

"Thank you, Peter. I just wanted you to know how I feel."

I laid my head on his shoulder as he pulled me to him, resting his chin on my head. We sat quietly for a few minutes. "What do you say we have a piece of that pie? I can put some tea on," he said, pushing the darker thoughts aside.

"Yes, let's do that. I think that's enough serious talk for one night."

The pie was just like Mom used to make. I'm not crazy over cake, even on my birthday, unless it's something really special, so I told her that instead of making me a cake, I'd just as soon have a pie. So that's what it was from then on.

"I'm dreading the long drive alone, Peter. It's going

to be lonely. I don't know whether it's worse to be the one leaving, or the one being left."

"Neither one is that great, is it?" he said.

"No...but I do think it's easier leaving than it is being left. I start dreading it an hour before I think you're going to leave and I have it worked into quite a lousy scene by the time you're ready to go." He blinked his eyes, looking surprised. "I mean my emotions are in a lousy mess." *Maybe I shouldn't have said so much.*

He studied me for a moment, processing what I'd just said. "I'm not working on Monday. How about if I come down and we could work in your garden?"

"Oh, would you, Peter? That would be lovely. I'll make some sandwiches and we can eat outside. That would be so nice. I'll have that to look forward to and maybe it won't seem so bad."

"I'll bring some snacks, now that I know what you like."

"Okay. Why don't you come for a late breakfast and I'll make some hash browns and omelets. That will give us a full stomach to work on."

So it was settled. He'd come Monday morning.

Chapter 14

Gardening

I WAS SITTING OUTSIDE HAVING MY COFFEE at seven thirty when Peter drove in.

"I just couldn't wait 'til any later," he said. "The soil was calling me. Or was it you calling?" he asked, merrily. "Anyway, I hope you don't mind that I came early."

"Mind? Do I look crazy?"

He shook his head, his eyes crinkling into a pleasant smile. "You're a case, Maggie, but I like you. I didn't think you'd mind. I'll go in and get myself a coffee and come and join you. That is, if you don't mind," he said, giving me a little bow and a sly grin.

"Quit the 'if you don't mind stuff,' I said, pretending to be annoyed. "As long as you're here, that's all I care about. I'm not a great hostess, as you've probably noticed," I said, hoping that he hadn't. "I like for all my company to do that, but especially you. Do you think you could handle that?" I ended, softly.

"If that's what you say, I'll try. It might take some

getting used to, but I'm game.

"I like your new cap," I said, when he came back and sat down. It had a Massey Harris tractor embroidered in a golden wheat field against a blue sky with fluffy white clouds. The cap, though, was the usual red he wore.

"I think you'd like anything that was growing as long as it wasn't a weed," he said, and I don't care as long as it's red. Red and yellow are my favorite colours and I guess I've got them both here. I have an old Massey Harris tractor that I got, oh, when I was sixteen or seventeen, and the cap reminded me of it. Maybe I'm a little bit like you and just like to be different. Some of the fellows tease me about wearing red, say it's sissy, but it doesn't bother me. I like it," he said. His boyish grin reminded me of Luke when I'd caught him eating a bag of chocolate chips.

It was the nicest morning coffee I'd had in a good long time. My feathered friends were singing a love song this morning. Yesterday, they were just gossiping about me.

We spent the day pulling weeds, putting peat moss around some things, and some rocks around the red maple on the corner by the nut trees.

I'd decided to make a macaroni salad instead of sandwiches. I'd made some air buns, and along with some pickles, it was a tasty lunch.

We finished the work around three o'clock and Peter asked if there was anything else I'd like done.

I'd been wondering what I could do in the orchard.

I wanted to put something down so I wouldn't have to mow around all the trees. I'd thought about landscape fabric and straw or sawdust. We decided to try the sawdust and took a drive to the garden outlet to get some.

It was four o'clock when we got back. "I think I'll go in and see what I can rummage up for supper, Peter. Would you like something to drink?"

"Yes, I'll come in and get a drink and then I think I'll start working in the orchard. I can get a start on it."

I decided we'd just have macaroni salad again. That's what I'd do if I was alone and busy.

When I called Peter, I had the plates made up with salad, toasted rolls, olives and dill pickles. "I hope you don't mind reruns," I said, while he was washing up. "I have them often, especially when I'm busy."

"I'm not sure I'd even notice as long as a certain pretty lady was sitting across the table from me," he said.

I looked around innocently. "Well, I don't see any pretty ladies, and I don't have time to go looking, but there is a lady here. Maybe she'll do."

Turning around, he kissed my forehead, giving me a light hug. "She'll more than do and don't forget that beauty is in the eye of the beholder. This looks good to me," he said, sitting down. "I'm quite used to eating the same thing for a few meals. Don't worry about me, as long as it's food, I'm not fussy."

Another point added, I thought. *Where am I at now?*

RHONDA CRONKHITE

I couldn't remember. Nor could I remember any negative ones either. *There must be at least a couple lurking about.*

We put the dishes in the sink and headed back to the orchard. Peter had one row of fabric down and some sawdust on it. It was much quicker with two working. I could hold the fabric while he rolled it out and cut it off and then we both shovelled the sawdust on that strip. In an hour and a half, it was finished. Now I'd just have to figure out something for an edging. Amos would have likely put four by fours around it. Maybe I could do that. I'd think about it.

"You've been a big help, Peter. I really appreciate it. Maybe I'll come down and help you some day. It's much more fun working together."

"My pleasure," he said. "Just think, I didn't have to get any meals today. Why don't we get a drink and take a walk around and see how it looks."

I poured some grape nectar and added some ginger ale in the plastic tumblers with covers and got a couple of straws. "Okay, let's go." On the way out, I turned the lights on in the crab apple tree and the lighthouse.

We strolled through the gardens, admiring the results of our hard work. The strawberries were almost ripe and they looked like they'd be a good size this year. "Next time you come, Peter, I'll make you some strawberry shortcake. I'll even use real cream, if you like."

"Sounds good to me," he said. "I grew up on real cream. We lived on a farm, remember?"

RHONDA CRONKHITE

"Yes, I do, and it's one of the places where I say it's worth eating the extra calories. I'll let you know when they're ripe." After a moment, I said, "They might be ripe tomorrow, you know."

He looked at me but said nothing, just put his arm around my waist, giving me a little squeeze.

Chapter 15

A Wonderful Drive

PETER CALLED AND SAID HE'D BE TAKING some logs to Millinocket, Maine, and wondered if I'd like to go. He would be leaving early in the morning

I'd been thinking about getting together with a couple of my friends but I hadn't confirmed yet. It didn't take any convincing to change my plans. "Sure, I could do that. Would you like me to bring some sandwiches and snack stuff? You can buy me a piece of pie, if you like."

"Okay, if that's what you want. You might want to bring a book and a pillow, in case you get bored or tired. It's a long ride and we'll be late getting back"

"Sounds good. I'll be ready."

I was up before my alarm went off and couldn't even sit still long enough to drink my coffee. I made salmon sandwiches with lettuce and shaved chicken with onion, pickles, lettuce, and cheese on sub buns. I grabbed some tortillas, cereal bars, and some juice boxes. Remembering the pumpkin chip cookies in the freezer, I got some of those, too.

I rushed around getting a pillow and one of my

furry blankets, along with a couple of blankets for the dogs. I put some treats, packets of food and a bowl for water in their bag, along with a couple bottles of water. I added my book and my knitting to the pile. I was making a scarf for Sebastian; he's into scarves.

I was ready when Peter drove in. We were soon loaded and on our way. After watching the scenery for a while, I decided to read.

"Do you read a lot?" Peter asked.

"Too much, probably. As soon as I learned to read, I couldn't get enough of it. Remember when the Bookmobile came to school and we could borrow some books? That was a big day for me. I can almost smell the polished wood. I always keep a book, or a few, on my nightstand and read until I start falling asleep."

"I like to read, too," he said. "I'd probably read the encyclopedia if there wasn't anything else around."

"Well, I don't have it that bad," I chuckled. "I like autobiographies and true crime, and Christian books, either fiction or biography, or study stuff. I read to Luke a lot when he was young. I was glad when he learned to read well enough himself, though. I enjoyed it, mind you, but he inherited a love for reading from both me and his dad and he could never get enough. He'd say, 'Just one more, Mom?' And he usually got it. Sometimes I read so long my tongue felt thick. That was quitting time."

"If you like reading out loud, you could read to me. What are you reading?"

"I thought I'd read Jeanette Oke's *Love Comes*

Softly. It's the first one in a series of probably ten books. She's my favourite Christian writer. I used to read another popular Christian author but her stories are so unbelievable. Rich girl meets poor boy, doesn't like him, falls in love, blah, blah, blah. Rich boy meets poor girl, she doesn't like him, falls in love, same old, same old. After I discovered Jeanette Oke, the other books seemed dead and dried up by the roots.

"I've read this series a few times and I still enjoy it. I can read some out loud and see if you like it." *I guess it's a man's story, too.* I remembered when Amos had woke in the middle of the night to find me starting the series yet another time. He asked if I'd read some to him and he was hooked. We read the whole series together, taking turns reading out loud. It had been fun.

"Sure, I'd like that," Peter said.

I read the 'About The Author' section and the 'Note To Readers' for Peter's benefit, and went on to Chapter One, 'The Grim Reaper,' where Marty finds herself out west, alone and scared, after her husband was killed when falling off his horse. She was surprised and taken aback when she received an unusual marriage proposal from a man named Clark Davis.

I read the first six chapters. "I'm getting sleepy, Peter. I think I'll take a break."

I locked the door before putting my pillow against the window, covering up with my blanket. I love my furry blankets, they hug you so nicely. I was soon fast asleep with Kiwi on my hip and Cinnamon snuggled up against me. Cookie was in his usual spot, on a blanket on the floor.

"So you decided to wake up," Peter said, much later, when I stirred. "I think it's about time to stop for a rest. I found your pumpkin cookies. I saved a couple for you. Are you getting hungry?"

"I'm always hungry when I'm driving," I said. "That's why I like to be well stocked."

We pulled in at the next rest area with three barking dogs impatiently waiting while we put their leashes on. It was chilly so we put our jackets on and stayed just long enough to eat and give the dogs a snack and a drink and time to pee.

Walking back towards the truck, I was surprised to notice that Peter was hauling a load of hornbeam. That looks like a nice load of hornbeam you have there," I exclaimed. "I wonder what they do with it? Luke likes it to make transfer boards. It's really beautiful when it's sanded. I guess they make tool handles out of it too, because it's so strong. That's why it's sometimes called 'ironwood'."

"Sounds like you've been doing your homework," he said. "They take quite a lot of it in Millinocket, I'm told."

"They're beautiful trees, too," I said. "I didn't know what they were called, but I'd been looking at them along the road for two or three years, trying to find one small enough to dig up, or pull up. The branches make me think of an umbrella. I couldn't believe my eyes or good luck when I noticed a couple small ones in the ditch right in front of my house. But it wasn't to be. One day when Luke was visiting, he noticed them, too. 'There's a hornbeam tree right there,' he said. Needless to say, I helped dig them up for him.

"So, if you ever come across one that's calling, 'Maggie, Maggie,' you can stop and get it for me."

"What will you come up with next?" he said, rolling his eyes.

I decided to knit for a while. I like to put a pin in where I start each time because it always surprises me how much I get done. By the time we got to the mill, I'd added another fifteen inches, with just a couple more feet needed to make it eighty-four inches; Sebastian likes his scarves long.

After the wood was unloaded, Peter asked if I was ready for a piece of pie. He said there was a country diner up the road a ways if I could wait awhile.

"Humph! Have you ever eaten there?" I asked.

"No, I've just heard how good it is."

"I've eaten there a few times and it's obvious to me, and judging from the smiles and nods of all the other diners as they dig into the piles of food that any elephant would drool over, shoving their taste buds in their pockets must have seemed like a fair exchange for size. I say that because the cardboard tasting potatoes, without a drop of salt, and the chili with huge chunks of meat and so much cayenne and chili powder that even the elephants would sniff at it, must have come from the same pot as mine. And my pockets are never large enough for my taste buds so I had no choice but to use mine. Yeah, some people don't care as long as their plate came from the zoo."

"You wouldn't be hard to please or anything, would you, Maggie?" Peter asked, not at all surprised to learn of another of my quirks.

"Possibly. Actually, probably," I said, as if just remembering I had been accused of such a crime in the past. "Maybe that's why Rose told me one time to shut up so she could enjoy her food," I said, hunching my shoulders and raising my eyebrows. But I had taken the hint. "I promise I won't embarrass you, Peter."

"Good," he said, sounding relieved. "I think I'll have a little rest here before we leave, if that's okay with you. I usually stop somewhere and take a little nap on the way. Age catching up with me, I guess."

"Sure, go ahead," I said "Here, take my pillow and I'll cover you up."

He turned towards me and put the pillow behind his head, leaning back against the door. I covered him up with my blanket.

After knitting for a few minutes, I said, "You don't look very comfortable, Peter. Why don't you put the pillow over here against my legs and put your feet up on the seat?" As usual, I was half turned in the seat with one leg curled underneath, and Kiwi on my lap.

"Mm, that sounds like a plan."

He got settled, curled up on his side, facing the front. I put my arm across his chest and sat looking at his handsome face, marvelling at how lucky I was. Before long, his breathing became slow and steady and I knew he was asleep.

RHONDA CRONKHITE

When he awoke an hour later, Kiwi was on his hip and I was fast asleep, my head lying on his shoulder, against the back of the seat, and my arm flung across his side.

Reaching back, he rubbed Kiwi's ear. "Do you suppose Sleeping Beauty is going to wake up, Miss Kii?" he said as he turned around, his lips lightly brushing mine in the process.

I roused and yawned. "Am I dreaming or what?"

"I wondered the same thing," Peter said, "but if I am, don't wake me, it's much too comfortable."

I sat up but continued to lean towards him, my arm still on his side. He took my hand, his face pretty close to mine. As I studied him, I had a sudden urge...*Dare I?* Returning his gaze, I contemplated. I brought his hand up and kissed it softly, still looking at him.

"Maggie, you're a tease. I thought you were going to kiss me for a moment," he said, disappointed, I thought.

"I decided I'm too old to be starting new tricks, Peter," I said, kissing him on the forehead. "Let's go get that pie, shall we?" Peter had sweet potato fries and a cheeseburger and I had lemon pie.

When we were on the road again, Peter said, "I'm wondering what's happening with Clark and Marty. Do you feel like reading some more?"

I read until it was too dark to see. I'd brought my book light but I didn't want to bother with it so we talked for a while.

Some time later, Peter asked if there were any

sandwiches left so I got them out and put a few on a napkin for him, saving a couple for myself, while we shared the last drink.

When we finished eating, I curled up on the seat with my pillow against the door again and covered up. Cinnamon got on my back ahead of Kiwi so Kii got on my shoulder.

"I'm not going to sleep, Peter, so you can talk to me, if you like. If I get sleepy, I might not answer but I like hearing someone talking softly. If you want to be really sweet, you can tell me when we go by the towns."

He laughed. "You don't want much do you? I'd say you might be a little spoiled," he said, squeezing my foot.

Soon, Peter was singing softly. The rhythmic sound of the tires against the pavement as I watched the coloured lights on the side mirror, the same as the ones on his other trucks, was soothing. I must have dozed because the next thing I knew, Peter was saying softly, "Going by White River Junction."

Chapter 16

Surprise

I WAS GOING TO LUKE'S ONE SUNDAY afternoon and, on impulse, decided I'd surprise Peter and showed up at his church. In the vestibule, I asked an usher if he'd mind getting Peter Weatherburn for me.

Peter came out, his look of surprise breaking into a big smile. "Maggie!" he beamed, "what a pleasant surprise!"

"I heard there was a man here I might be interested in," I said, letting my eyes dance a little mischievously.

He looked puzzled for a second and then said, "You are a brat, Maggie," but his shining eyes said that I was anything but. "Shall we go in then?"

"I just thought, Peter," I began, suddenly realizing that I'd been a bit presumptuous. "Do the folks here know about me?"

"Some of them do, and the rest soon will," he said, as he escorted me in to his seat.

I went out to dinner with Peter and his family and then to Luke's for supper. It had turned out to be a wonderful day! The surprised look on Peter's face had been priceless and he hadn't seemed the least bit put out by my unexpected appearance.

After that, I always went to church with him on Sundays and out to dinner with the family, but I took my own car as far as his place. Our relationship was definitely getting more serious. I couldn't imagine life without Peter now. It made my heart feel pretty light the way his face lit up when I arrived each Sunday morning. His family seemed comfortable with our relationship, too. We even invited Luke and the boys over for pie one Sunday evening and after that, it became a ritual...one that I loved.

I couldn't suppress a smile when I thought about Ben's reaction when he'd first seen Luke. Ben had stood mesmerized as Nicholas helped his dad out of the car. When Luke was settled in his chair, Ben said, "Can you walk?" To which Luke replied, "You must be Ben, the little fellow Mom is always talking about. No, I can't walk. I had an accident and fell a long ways and now I have to use this chair."

"Are you Maggie's boy?" he asked, his eyes bulging wide as his jaw dropped to his chest. Putting his hands on his hips, he went on, "She didn't say her boy can't walk," his voice registering shock.

"Maybe she forgot, do you suppose? Sometimes when I wake up, I forget for a minute, but then my old legs remind me. I bet I can still play some games with you. What do you like to play?" Luke asked, reaching out to tousle his hair, as Ben looked at his arms, as if surprised that at least they worked.

"I like playing pick-up sticks and basketball. Daddy got a net just for me, "he said, "but you couldn't do that, you can't walk."

"Well, I don't think I'd be very good at pick up sticks but I'll bet I could throw the basketball if it fits you. What do you say we try it some time?"

"Maybe," Ben said, looking doubtful.

Luke tousled Ben's hair again as he wheeled away, smiling, as if to say 'I can see why Mom think he's so cute.' Ben stood gazing, clearly not knowing what to think. Seeing his look of befuddlement I went to him. "I see you've met my son. It doesn't seem like long ago since he was your size, Ben."

"That must have been a long time ago. And he can't walk," he said, shaking his head.

"I should have told you, Ben. I guess I just didn't think about it, but he's okay. When bad things happen, we have to make the best of it. Like when your gramma died. You just had to keep going, right?"

"I guess, so," he said, shrugging.

"Now let's go meet my grandsons. "Come on, Marissa,'" I said, taking her hand when she came to meet us. "You'll like them."

When I introduced them to Nicholas, Ben said, "You sure look like your dad," looking him up and down, as if checking to see that Nick was actually standing on his legs. To Sebastian, he said, "How tall are you anyway?" while Marissa smiled prettily when I introduced her as my princess. Sebastian and Nicholas chuckled as we left to find Grampa.

"Nan's in her glory now, isn't she Nick?" I heard Sebastian say.

"I'm sure she is," Nicholas replied. Ben was beaming. He had just made some new friends.

The folks at church were the only people I'd met who had known both Peter and Sandi, besides Judah. There were a couple of ladies who Peter said had been good friends with Sandi. They were a little reserved at first, but seemed to be feeling more comfortable. For the most part, everyone was friendly and seemed genuinely happy for Peter. After all, grief and loss is a very real part of life, and they'd seen lots of that.

I was beginning to secretly wonder when he would pop the question. I felt sure he would. I had my answer ready; I'd just smile and say, "I'd be honoured to be your wife, Peter." Yes, I was expecting it, and in all honesty, getting a little anxious. We seemed so perfect together, and I knew that Peter enjoyed my company as much as I did his. Life really was good!

Chapter 17

That Rascal, Ben

WE DECIDED WE'D TAKE A SATURDAY and just have some fun. We stopped at Luke's for a few minutes before going to Tuckerbox, the family restaurant where Sebastian worked part-time. I was pleased to see that he was working that day, looking sharp in his black pants and shirt. He looked surprised to see us, then gave me a hug and said, all professional like, "And where would you like to sit, Ms. LaHaye?"

"Any place is fine. All I can see is the man sitting across from me, so it really doesn't matter," I said, playfully.

"I think, Nan," he said, "as Grampie would say, you've got it worse than you had it when you took it," pretending to whisper, but loud enough for Peter to hear.

"Perhaps," I agreed, smiling smugly. Peter couldn't quite keep a straight face.

We decided to have coffee and a piece of pie. Tuckerbox is known for good coffee, although to me, it's hard to beat good old instant Maxwell House. I guess they have free Wi-Fi because there were lots of young folks hanging out with laptops, but the atmosphere was still very nice.

Peter asked if I'd like to take the White River Flyer out to Thetford and back. It would be a two and a half hour ride. The train left at noon, so we'd have to get cracking if we wanted to catch it. It sounded good to me.

Peter got our tickets and we found a seat halfway back just as the conductor started down the aisle. The first stop was the Cedar Circle Farm, an organic educational farm. I could have wandered around half the day, looking at the flowers and vegetables. I bought a loaf of brown bread from the kitchen and discovered that they offer cooking classes. That might be interesting sometime.

Peter bought a bag of apples. I gulped in surprise when he ate the whole apple, core and all. He winked. I guess those little hard pieces don't get stuck in his throat.

The next stop was the Montshire Science Museum. I loved it there, too. It reminded me of Epcot Center in Florida. I especially liked the scaled model of the Solar System. We only saw part of it because it's so large; Pluto is a two-mile walk away.

We both were rather quiet on the way back, enjoying the scenery along the Connecticut River, with the trees dressed in various shades of yellow, orange, red and brown. We even got to see the White Mountain foothills. It had been such a lovely afternoon, romping around, hand in hand, enjoying all the sights. Love is such a fair player, changing the looks of the whole world, whether looking through young eyes or old. The world was looking pretty beautiful to me.

We headed off to visit Peter's family, stopping at Zeke and Ruby's first. They were working in the gardens so we chatted outside awhile.

When we arrived at Kendra and Arnie's, Ben and Marissa came running out. "Oh, Grampa, I didn't know you were coming," Ben squealed, his face lighting up.

"I wanted to surprise you," Peter said, sounding almost as excited as the children.

"Did you remember the candy?"

"Let me see," he said, pretending to search his pocket. Sure enough there were two peppermints. He gave one to each of them.

"Thanks Grampa, I love you," Ben squealed.

"I love you too," Marissa said shyly.

"I love you, too, you little turkeys" Peter said, squeezing Ben tighter and putting his arm around Marissa's shoulder.

Kendra served tea and chocolate doughnuts she'd made that morning. Arnie had gone to the office for a while.

When we were ready to leave, they came out with us. While Kendra was talking to Peter, Ben saw his chance to speak to me.

"You remembered, didn't you?" he said, looking at my finger. "I didn't tell." he whispered.

"I sure did, Ben. I'm glad you told me about that."

"So are you gonna be our new gramma?" he asked, his voice sounding like he might not mind the idea, after all.

Peter was talking to Kendra, but I knew he could participate in one conversation and listen to another as well. "Let's take a little walk," I said, taking their hands while walking towards the apple tree in the side yard. When I thought we were out of earshot, I stopped and knelt down on one knee so I was at Ben's level, looking directly at him. Speaking softly, I said, "Your grandpa and I are very good friends, Ben, but we haven't talked about getting married. Why do you ask? Do you want a new gramma?"

"Well, I don't know. Can you read good? Can you sing?" he asked.

"Oh, I can read pretty good and I can make some weird noises that sounds a little like singing," I said.

With one eyebrow raised, he asked, "Well, do you let kids eat cookie dough and lick the batter out of the bowl? Can I pick your flowers?"

Rescuing me from that one, Marissa chimed in merrily, "I wouldn't mind if we got a new gramma."

"You're such a sweetie, Marissa," I said.

Looking at both of them, I said, "I'm sure your gramma was good to you. She couldn't help it with such cute little guys, now could she?" Marissa beamed and Ben couldn't help but smile a little. "I wouldn't worry about it though if I were you. If your grandpa ever decides to get married again, I'm sure it will be to a nice lady who would be really nice to you, too. I paused for a moment. "I think I have some little fun tricks up my sleeve for when I have little fellows around, too," I said, giving Ben a conspiratorial wink. His eyes brightened. "You must miss your gramma a lot."

They nodded. "Grandpa misses her, too. I heard him tell Mommy," was Ben's reply.

"We always miss someone we love when they have to leave us, Ben. But you were blessed to have her and it sounds like you have lots of good memories. That's wonderful."

"I guess so," he said, not quite convinced. "Do you love Grampa?"

"Ben, you shouldn't ask questions like that," chided big sister, Marissa.

Thinking quickly, I said, "I like your grampa a lot, Ben. I think he's a very nice man, don't you?"

"Oh yes, I do" he said. "I was just wondering what you thought."

"You're pretty smart, Ben. I think I like you," I said, taking his face in my hands. "You don't mind saying what you're thinking. That's a good way to be, you know."

"I hear everyone else talking about it," he said.

"Ben!" Marissa gasped. "You're not supposed to tell everything! Mommy won't like it." Looking at me, she said, "I like you, Maggie. I don't care if you're our gramma or not. But I wouldn't mind if you were," she finished shyly.

"Oh, Marissa, you're a doll," I said, letting go of her hand and putting my arm around her, giving her a little squeeze.

"It's okay, Ben. Little boys are supposed to ask questions. Now, let's go see what Mommy and Grampa are up to."

As we prepared to leave, Peter hugged the children. I hugged Marissa and ruffled Ben's hair. "You have lovely children, Kendra," I said. "I think Ben will make a good lawyer, he knows how to reword his questions to get to the bottom of a thing."

"He is pretty smart," Peter said, his eyes shining with pride.

Ben looked from Grampa to me, and back to Grampa. "Maggie likes you, Grampa. She said she does."

Peter looked at me, started to chuckle and then looked from Kendra to the children.

"Well, there's nothing wrong with liking a boy's grampa, now, is there? Especially a boy as nice as Ben," I said, giving Ben a conspiratorial little wink. I got a real smile that time.

Chapter 18

Proposal At Last!

I THINK YOU'VE WON BEN'S HEART," Peter said.

"He's a little sweetie, isn't he? And Marissa is such a darling."

When he shut the car engine off, he slid over beside me, putting his arm on the back of the seat. I didn't move from my usual position, with one leg curled underneath myself. He was silent for a moment. "I heard you talking to Ben," he said. "I'm an awful eavesdropper, you know."

Where's this going? I don't especially like being eavesdropped upon. "Maybe you're like my mother. My nephew said she had bionic ears," I said, laughing softly, pretending it didn't matter.

"I was going to say you were pretty wise, but maybe you were just being cagey," he said. I couldn't tell if he was being funny or accusing me of something so I made no response. "And then I thought what a great gramma you would make for Ben. I guess you'd have to be a Weatherburn to be his gramma, though, wouldn't you? Hmm. Maggie

Weatherburn, that has a nice ring to it, don't you think?"

Goodness, what am I supposed to say to that?

"What do you think about being Maggie Weatherburn?"

I did hear right. Didn't I? "It would depend on how I'd get to be Maggie Weatherburn, and for what reason. Do you mean so I could be a gramma to Ben and Marissa? And to Pete and Lizzie?" I asked innocently.

"Well, I guess that would go along with it, but I was kinda liking the idea of you being Maggie Weatherburn."

"Uh, and just what are you suggesting, Peter?" It might be 2012 and I was a lot more spontaneous than I had been back when Sam had proposed to me, but I wasn't going to let him off that easily.

I don't believe in assuming anything that's written between the lines either. A man ought to say exactly what he means. But then I don't think anyone would have ever said I was 'easy' either.

I thought about when Sam had first asked me out. He was like Peter in a lot of ways, one being that he was the most popular fellow in our group, the one that all the girls were secretly, or not so secretly, hoping to capture.

I was the last one on the scene, but I knew a prize when I saw it and this fellow was it. He had the character to go with the looks. Now did I have what it took to get him to look my way?

RHONDA CRONKHITE

The Unexpected Love

Apparently so. A couple of months later, we were having a weekend convention at my church and the folks from Sam's church were visiting. The boys were staying in a camp a few miles away. Since Sam had a half ton with a cap on it, he was taking the boys over, but the girls were going along for the ride. He'd bring us back before returning to the camp himself.

Everyone except Sam's best friend, Ken, got in the back of the truck. There was no seat belt law back then. When the boys were dropped off, Ken came back and said, "Sam wants Maggie to get in the front, and Rose can come, too."

I can't say that I wasn't thrilled to hear those words. Wasn't that just what I'd been holding my breath for? But it didn't seem like proper etiquette to me. After a moment's hesitation, I said, "If he wants me to go up there, he'll have to come and ask me himself."

No one could believe I was saying that. There wasn't a girl there who wouldn't have been out of the back and in the front quicker than you could say "scat." The girls were all saying, "Go on, Maggie, he wants you up there," but I stood my ground.

Ken, with a look of disbelief, reluctantly went back to the cab. After a couple of minutes, Sam came back, smiling nervously. "Maggie, would you and Rose like to get in the front?" I sure didn't need to be asked twice.

I must admit that I was always glad I'd stood my ground. Some things just should be done right. Perhaps Sam had that moment in mind when, a few weeks later, he sent me a graduation picture, and on the back he'd written: "To a girl who is pleasingly different."

So I wasn't filling in any blanks for Peter either.

He took my hand, looking at me with a mixture of love and anxiety. "I think you're already a gramma to my grandchildren, Maggie. You're the best thing that's happened to our family since...in a long time. I think my grandkids already love you almost as much as I do."

My heart was getting ready for some acrobatics, but he still hadn't got around to Maggie Weatherburn. Well, he had said the love word for the first time, but...

"The more time we spend together, the more I want to be with you. We seem so right together. Would you marry Ben's grampa and change your name to Weatherburn?" he asked, with just a hint of a smile. "What I mean is, will you marry me, Maggie LaHaye?" For once, there was no teasing in his eyes.

My heart was doing somersaults in a spring rain, not caring if it fell down into the mud. "Oh, that's what you were meaning. I'd love to be a gramma to the kids, they need a gramma. And I have a feeling I'd like being their grampa's wife, too." More softly, I said, "I'd be honoured to be your wife, Peter. I think I've loved you from the first day you drove in my yard. That would make me about the happiest woman alive."

He moved towards me, my leg flew out from underneath me and I was in his arms. "I'd be proud to have you for my wife, Maggie," he said, his voice

RHONDA CRONKHITE

kind of rough, as he buried his face in my hair and then his lips were on mine. Time stood still for a few moments; the whole world stopped and Peter and I were the only two people in it. When our lips finally parted, he put his forehead against mine.

"Peter!...I love you," I whispered, breathlessly.

"Maggie..." was all he said for a moment. "I can't believe how fortunate I am to have found you. You're such a sweetheart, Maggie. I never thought life would feel this good again."

My heart was pounding. I moved back so I could look at him. "Nor did I," I said. "I'm so glad you decided to stop in that day."

"Yeah, me too. I really didn't plan to ask you out so soon though. I was a little nervous. But you made me feel welcome and I didn't get any negative vibes, so I guess I got brave" he said.

"And why would you be nervous, Peter Weatherburn? Any sensible woman would be quite pleased to see you driving in her yard." *Everything about him is lovable and desirable. Not lustful, but what any woman in her right mind would hope for. Someday, I'll tell him that.*

He smirked. "You don't mean to tell me that you'd been hoping a certain fellow would show up, do you?"

"I wouldn't put it quite that way," I said, smiling shyly, "but I did think you'd likely make a good friend, if you ever knew you needed one."

"I guess it was a good decision then," he said, his

face radiant and eyes sparkling. *Were there tears trying to find their way to the surface?*

"You never once caught me batting my eyes at you, though, like a few others I've noticed, now did you?" I said, batting my eyes ever so slightly.

"You batting your eyes at a man? That would be a first, wouldn't it?" He chuckled. "I think sometimes my friendly nature gets me in trouble. But I don't dislike my own company enough to let myself get tangled up with someone who would turn my life upside down. There are worse things than being alone, I think."

"My sentiments exactly. I must admit I was pretty excited for an old grandmother when you drove in that day. I know you don't do things lightly, but still..."

"So would you like to come with me to pick out a ring?"

"Oh, I'd love that. You say when."

"How about tomorrow, then?"

And that was that. We went ring shopping on Monday, the next day being Sunday and our church day. I hardly dared hope for white gold, I didn't know what price range Peter had in mind. So I was thrilled when we chose an Asscher cut topaz diamond in a white gold setting. It's a rather flat stone, a larger one in the center with three smaller ones of graduating sizes on either side. The matching band was set with seven of the smaller stones. It was totally different than anything I'd seen before, and I loved it. Besides, topaz is my birth stone.

The next day, I found myself holding my hand up, admiring my ring every few minutes as I went about my work. It was exquisite and what it stood for was...I couldn't think of a word good enough...splendid, heavenly, glorious all rolled into one. I was certainly loving my new life.

I thought about how Peter and Luke had connected rather quickly. Since Peter had offered to help Nicholas with his wheeler, they had spent a lot of time together, Peter often helping Luke with mechanics. He'd done some welding on Luke's utility trailer, too.

Nick had even spent the night at Peter's once when they hadn't got the job finished. Luke had commented to me about how easy Peter is to talk to. I was very happy for Luke.

We had all enjoyed the Sunday evenings we'd spent at Peter's with his family. Being the same age, Luke and Zeke had naturally gravitated to each other. Luke had helped Zeke with designing his three-level deck and I noticed that Zeke usually helped Luke get in the car, giving Kate and the boys a break.

Sebastian works mostly in special care, having taken his training when he worked for me. When his dad's worker couldn't make it, he'd take over with Luke's care, never blinking at the need to provide catheters, showers, or even bowel care. I don't think I could have done that for my mom, not at the tender age of sixteen. He works a lot of hours, supporting himself and Holly while she's in university and then he plans to train for an RN. Naturally, he can find lots to talk with Zeke and Ruby about.

I liked Peter's family a lot. They'd all been wonderful to me, especially Zeke and Ruby. Kendra had seemed a little uncomfortable on our first meeting, but before the day was out, I think she realized that I wasn't a threat to their happy family.

And the children - I loved them all, but especially the little rascal, Ben. He was a comical fellow, saying whatever popped into his head.

Yes, life was really wonderful.

Chapter 19

Exciting News

WE COULDN'T WAIT TO SHARE THE NEWS with our families. We invited them all to Peter's place for a barbecue.

Ben and Marissa came running to meet us, Ben soon being scooped up by his grampa while Marissa threw her arms around my waist. Pete and Liz were hanging back, waiting for Peter to greet them.

After dinner, Peter spoke, his voice catching. "We're glad you could all come today. We wanted you to be the first to know that Maggie and I have decided to get married. You've probably figured out that we've fallen quite in love and a little birdie said you might not even be surprised." His family looked from one to the other, apparently wondering who had let the cat out of the bag, but no one admitted to such a thing.

"We know it will be different for you, but we both love you all, and want you to feel welcome to come to our home anytime, the same as you always have. We're not sure where we'll live but what's important is that we have our families.

"I know I could never take the place of Luke's dad or step dad, nor would I want to, but I do feel honoured to be your friend," he said, looking at Luke. "Sebastian and Nicholas, you're special to me, already.

"To my family," he hesitated for a second, "Maggie wants me to tell you that you don't have to try and not mention Sandi. She was your mother. She wants you to remember her. There's nothing to hide. I still love your mom," he said softly, biting his lip as he looked off into the distance, "and always will," he finished, his voice trailing away. He hesitated and I put my hand on his shoulder, rubbing it a couple of times before letting it rest. He looked at me and I nodded my encouragement. His voice was a bit unsteady as he continued, "and Maggie still loves Sam and Amos, but we have room for each other. There's always room for love. I couldn't have found a better partner than Maggie, and I hope you all learn to love her as much as I do," he finished, looking around at our families.

When the clapping died down, I spoke. "I can't say how happy I am. Peter is such a wonderful man and he has such a lovely family, too," I said, taking the time to look at each of them. I knew my face was radiant and my heart felt about ready to burst. "And I'm so happy that my boys like Peter, too. Although I couldn't imagine anyone not liking Peter," I said, while some giggles were heard and everyone relaxed.

Ben squealed, "So do I have to call you Gramma?" You could hear the breaths drawn in, and held, but I was quick to respond.

"You can call me whatever you like, Ben. Mostly though, I'd like to be your friend. You can come for sleepovers, too. My grandsons call me 'Nan.' Maybe you'd like to call me 'Nan,' too. You can ask Sebastian and Nick, they'll tell you that I make a pretty good Nan. I can read to you and probably sing some silly songs, too."

"Really? What kind of silly songs?" he asked, his eyes wide.

"Come here," I said, without taking time to think. As he came towards me, I said "I'll show you how I do it," as I picked him up, putting him on my hip and twirling around.

"Let's see, it goes something like this," and Peter, with laughter ringing in his voice said, "Be careful, Ben. You might get more than you bargained for." I started to sing, continuing to twirl around slowly.

Oh my darling, Oh my darling

Oh my darling little Ben

You're the sweetest little boy

That I've seen since I don't know when - to the tune of "My Darling Clementine."

"I used to sing that to Sebastian and Nicholas when they were little tykes like you. But you decide what you want me to be and that's just what I'll be."

"What did you sing to Sebastian and Nicholas? Cause if I'm the sweetest boy, what were they?" Everyone roared with laughter.

"Well, let's see," I said, thinking for a moment. "Come here Nick, we have to show Ben." Looking embarrassed, Nicholas started towards me slowly. I put Ben down and met Nick. I said I guessed that Nicholas was too big to pick up now so I took his hand and put my other arm around his waist as I sang,

Oh my darling, Oh my darling

Oh my darling Nickie boy

You're the sweetest little grandson

And you're Nanny's pride and joy

And Sebastian's, let me think." Sebastian came to meet me, taking my hand and putting his other arm around my shoulder, as I put mine around his waist. "It goes like this" he said, and he began singing as we danced,

Oh my darling, oh my darling

Oh my darling Nanny mine

I gazed up into his face, my eyes glistening with tears very near to spilling over. My sweet grandson, proudly declaring his love for me. I'd sung the song a million times, but no one had ever sung it to me.

You're the sweetest of the Nannies

I'll love you 'til the end of time.

"Sebastian!" I whispered. "You're adorable. I love you so much," I said, reaching up and kissing his cheek.

"I love you too, Nan. You're the best Nan I could have had," he finished, his voice faltering.

Regaining my composure, I said, "Yes that's how it goes, Ben," and I began singing

Oh my darling, oh my darling

The Unexpected Love

Oh my darling Jonathan

You're the sweetest little Jonnie

You're the sweetest boy I've found

"Thank you, Sebastian," I said, when we'd finished. "That's what we called Sebastian when he was little," I said to the others.

"My dad was always saying silly rhymes to us, and I guess it rubbed off on me. I even sing that song to my dogs, so I guess I'm a little silly, too."

Walking over to Peter, I smiled playfully. "And what did I hear you say, Peter, about getting more than you bargained for?" As I held my hand out, he got up, a sheepish look firmly planted on his face.

"Peter was jealous one day when he caught me singing that song to my dogs," I said, "so I..."

"I was not jealous," he said, rolling his eyes.

"Was, too," I countered. "He was jealous so I had to make it up to him," I said, putting one hand on his waist and the other on his shoulder.

Oh my darling, Oh my darling

Oh my darling Peter dear

You're the sweetest man I've seen around

And I am oh so glad you're here

I sang, looking at him with all the love I felt, as we danced slowly.

Oh my darling, Oh my darling,

Oh please love me Peter dear

For my life would be so worthless

If I found that you weren't here

RHONDA CRONKHITE

It looked like stars in his eyes, but maybe it was tears begging to escape.

Oh my darling, Oh my darling,

Oh please love me lest I cry

For if you should up and leave me

Then I might just up and die (saying the "and die" in my lowest voice.)

Then to my surprise, Peter began

Oh my darling, Oh my darling

Oh my darling Maggie dear, as my eyes wanted to overflow again

I don't think that I could stand it

So I guess I'll keep you here

I couldn't hide the pleasure I felt. "You are such a prize, Peter," I gushed. More softly I whispered, "And you're my prize, don't forget."

"Yes! Yes!" Ben shrieked, jumping up and down as he clapped his hands. "I'd like to call you Nan. I like that!" he almost shouted, his little face beaming with joy.

Zeke was beaming, too, as he looked at Ben. "I think you just passed the test, Maggie." My heart was purring. Everyone clapped, the pleasant laughter rippling through the air. Even the ducks seemed excited, quacking loudly.

I looked around at this rather new family blending so easily together, it seemed...a person looking from the outside might assume we had always been together...well, almost.

RHONDA CRONKHITE

When the excitement began to wind down, Zeke and Ruby came over to Peter. Zeke hugged his dad. "We're so happy for you, Dad. Maggie is lovely. We love her already." Ruby echoed Zeke's feeling. "We're all so happy for you, Dad."

"I'm pretty happy myself," Peter said, his face radiant. My heart warmed watching him, seeing the love in his eyes. "I'm so glad you all like her. I was a little worried about Kendra, but Maggie knew how to handle her."

"Well, what's not to like, Dad? She's wonderful," Zeke said.

They both hugged and congratulated me, admiring the ring. "I'm so happy to be a part of your family and you've all made me feel so welcome," I said, trying to keep my emotions from running away.

Then Kendra was giving her dad a big hug, with Arnie beside her. "I'm so happy for you, Dad. I really am." She stood back, letting her hands slide down to her father's forearms. "You're right, Dad, we have room in our hearts for everyone. We'll just be one big happy family. It's so nice to see you truly happy." She hesitated and there were tears welling up in her eyes when she spoke. "You and Maggie make a lovely couple, Dad. I really like her."

"Oh, Kendra!" Peter said softly, as he hugged her tight. "You don't know what that means to me, Sweetheart. I sure feel like Maggie is a real treasure."

Arnie nodded. "We're very happy for you, Dad."

I made my way to Luke and Kate. "We're so happy

for you, Mom," Luke said. "Peter is a perfect gentleman. I like him a lot."

Peter, coming over, heard his name. "What's that I hear about me?" he asked.

Luke said, "I was just telling Mom how happy we are for her, for both of you. You're a great guy, Peter."

"Thank you, Luke" Peter said softly. "It's rather odd, but it feels like we've known each other forever. We've all grown so close."

"It is kinda funny," Luke said thoughtfully. "I've often wondered what my dad was like. Mom's told me lots about him, and she's always made him sound so perfect, I couldn't compare him to anyone I knew. But you seem to fit the picture I've had in my mind of what I've thought he must have been like."

"Thank you, Luke. That's a real compliment. I could never take your dad's place, but I'd be honoured to fill in for him." Luke nodded. "Anything you'd talk to your own dad or step dad about, I want you to feel free to ask me. Your other step dad, I mean."

Luke was clearly touched. He couldn't speak as his eyes filled with tears. Peter bent towards him, hugging him tight. "We're family now and I love you, Luke."

"I love you too, Peter," Luke said, choking back the emotion. "And you've already made me feel cared for like a father would. I might forget and even call you 'Dad' sometimes," he said as a smile spread across his face.

"That would make me very happy." Peter smiled lovingly at his soon-to-be stepson who seemed to have not had the father-son relationship he so craved.

By now, Sebastian and Nick had joined the group, smiling as they looked on. They hadn't seen their dad so happy in a long time. Kate and I were both wiping our eyes. My heart had broken for Luke so many times. He'd had so much to deal with and he'd been so strong. I was very proud of him.

"You're a good man, Peter," Luke continued. "My mom's always been very special in my eyes, but you've lit a spark that I don't remember seeing before. No offence, Mom," he grinned.

"None taken, Sweetie," I assured him.

"Amos and I had some rough times and some good times. We'd become friends the year before I got hurt. I don't know whether he changed or if I did. Maybe we both did. Mom says he changed, but I can't remember. I do wish it could have always been that way. We can't undo the past, but I'm looking forward to the future," he said, his face glowing. "I'm glad you found us, Peter."

As our families were getting ready to leave, Zeke spoke; "I think we're all tickled about our new family. We're a pretty lucky lot, if you ask me."

Peter came over to me, putting his arm around my shoulder and kissing my cheek. I slipped my arm around his waist.

Looking at Luke, Zeke grinned. "I've always wished I had a brother, but since we've gotten to know each other, I think maybe this is what brothers feel like. I think maybe you'll do," he said happily.

Luke laughed. "I guess that's a compliment Zeke...and I think I'll have to do. I don't think you're getting any more than a stepbrother, not with our parents reaching for sixty."

The crowd erupted in hilarious laughter. Peter and I looked at one another, he biting his lip and eyes twinkling as I squeezed him a bit tighter for a moment.

"You got one on me there, Luke," Zeke admitted. "I sure am glad that Dad got his glasses out and found your mom before some other bloke did. If one has to have a stepmother at my age, it might as well be a good one," he said, grinning like a Cheshire cat while they burst out laughing again. "Actually, you might say she's been a breath of fresh air around here." Winking at me, he said, "Thank you, Maggie. If you can keep my dad this happy, I might even call you Momma Maggie once in a while," he grinned, a tormenting grin just like his dad's. I was glowing inside, loving Zeke already.

Smiling at her brother, Kendra said "I couldn't have said it any better, Zeke."

I squeezed Peter a little tighter as he kissed the top of my head, keeping his head against mine.

Before leaving, Ben came running up to me. "Does that mean you're our new gramma?" he asked, excitedly.

"I think that's just what it means, Ben. And I'm so

happy about it. I can hardly wait," I said.

"Me, too!" he squealed, his eyes shining.

When everyone had left and things were back in order, Peter sat down in his armchair. "Come sit with me, Maggie" he said, patting his lap.

I looked at him hesitantly. "Do you know how much I weigh?" I asked, hedging.

"I'd like to find out" he said. "I think I can hold you."

I walked over to him and sat down cautiously, shyly. He gently turned my shoulders so that I was facing him. "You're lovely, Maggie. Do you know that?" he asked.

"Only if you tell me" I answered coyly.

"You are a force to be reckoned with, Maggie, but I think I like you."

Taking his face in my hands, I said, "You'd better like me, Mr. Weatherburn, or I may have to return the order for a gramma for Ben." Shaking his head, he said, "Come on, Gramma, I'll drive you home then. How's that?"

Chapter 20

Planning

DURING THE RIDE, PETER ASKED, "So how are we going to do things, Maggie? We're both used to living alone. We'll have to figure out how we want to share the work. What would you like for me to do? Or should I say, what do you like doing?"

"I don't know," I said, thoughtfully. "Right now, I might be foolish enough to say I'd wait on you hand and foot, just to be able to wake up to your handsome face every morning," I said, rolling my eyes in jest. He looked like he didn't know whether to believe that blarney or not.

"I'm also nearing sixty, so I've learned a thing or two. I don't think it's wise to start relationships, either marriage or otherwise, on any false pretenses, doing things you won't feel comfortable doing for a lifetime. Maybe it will take us awhile to figure things out, but here's the deal. I'll tell you exactly how I feel, if you promise to do the same. We might not agree on everything, but at least we'll know what the other is thinking, and we can work on it."

"Okay, I can do that. Who's first?"

"You can be first," I said, but before he had a chance to open his mouth, I hurried on, "after I say this one thing. Back when we were young, things were different. Typically, the woman stayed at home and looked after almost everything and the man went out and worked all day. When you really sit back and look at that, though, the man worked all day, eight or ten hours, and the woman worked from the time she got up until she went to bed. I certainly didn't mind doing it at the time. Today, things are quite different. Women either have to, or choose to have a job, too. I think in that case, the work at home needs to be shared.

"I'm speaking in general here, but in most cases, women wear themselves out and it's probably no wonder that by the time they get to bed, all they want to do is go to sleep. It'll soon be time to get up and start the whole thing all over again.

"Even when the woman is a full-time homemaker, I don't think a man should leave his dirty clothes lying on the floor. He's very capable of putting them in the laundry hamper. He's capable of taking his dishes to the sink. I think it's much nicer being a man's sweetheart than his slave."

"And the crazy thing is that women start things off that way because they're madly in love with Prince Charming and they like doing all that stuff for him. But by the time they have a kid or two, they're resenting it. And he's enjoying it too much to change. *Hey, what's different all of a sudden,* he wonders? Life seems the same to him...he gets up and goes to work and comes home to supper ready, at least most of the time, and now there's a few sweet little pumpkins to love, besides. He just can't understand why his wife is so tired all the time.

With us, it's different. Our kids are grown, I'm not working, you're semi-retired, and as you say, we're both kinda used to doing our own thing."

More softly, I said, "I don't think you're like that, Peter. I'm just telling you what I've observed. Right now, I love making dinner for you, and you seem to enjoy doing the same for me. I'd like it to always be that way.

I know it's not just men. Sometimes, it's the other way around. I've seen lots of women leading their men around on leashes, wanting him to be a dog one minute, grovelling at her feet and then expecting him to have a backbone the next. It's all pretty sick, if you ask me."

The shocked look on Peter's face brought me to my senses.

"Goodness, I didn't mean to babble on like that. You may have decided by now you want this ring back," I said, concerned that I'd been too outspoken.

He took a long breath. "I'm glad you told me how you feel, Maggie. I've never heard it put quite that bluntly before, but I can see where you're coming from. I'm just glad that I've never, well at least I don't think I have, ever been guilty of being the kind of jerk you seem to be referring to."

I smiled, a rather wobbly smile.

"Just give me a moment here to...to...think...to digest all that," Peter said. "I've never heard of a woman quite brave enough to say all that in one breath, especially to the man I've heard her calling Prince Charming." *Was he teasing?* I couldn't read his expression. "I must say, if I thought you were in any way insinuating that I might be in need of some of those alterations, I...well, I'd probably have to go home and do some thinking."

"Okay, Peter. Let me just qualify that spiel. If I thought you were any of those things, I wouldn't even be sitting here. Then again, likely if I put on my lecturing cap every day, you wouldn't be sitting there, either." *Goodness! Sometimes I do get carried away!*

"Now that I've opened my big mouth and spouted all that off, if you can listen to just one more thing I have to say, maybe you'll understand. I never thought I'd be facing the decision of marriage again, but I've said that if I ever was, my yardstick would be pretty stiff."

Looking at him for a moment, and choosing what I hoped were words that revealed the true depth of my feelings, I forged on. "Peter...I want you to know that I realize what a good man you are. I feel very privileged to be the lady you've chosen to share your life with." I couldn't resist adding, "I do realize that you had other choices," the gleam in my eyes taking the edge off the moment. "What I'm about to say may help you to really believe that. I've said that if I was ever in the position to see a man again, he'd have just three chances before striking out."

RHONDA CRONKHITE

Peter's eyes widened.

"There are things that can be negotiated, and there are things that are deal breakers. There are things a person can change, can work on, and there are things that will never change.

"So if I saw something I really didn't think I could live with, I'd tell a man that. He may not have thought of it before, so you can't blame him for that. I'm sure there are things about me that some men wouldn't be able to deal with either. So, I'd tell him how I felt. That's number one.

If it happened again, I'd remind him. That's number two.

"If I saw it again, there would be one more warning. I guess that makes it four strikes, and that's one too many, but if it happened again, the game would be over. No more negotiations. It wouldn't be worth it - to me or to him. There's no sense living in a tug of war. He'd have to go find someone else who'd put up with his foolishness," I said, hearing the edge in my voice again.

Feeling almost drained, I finished, my voice barely above a whisper, "I've been keeping track, Peter, and I haven't seen anything about you that I don't love."

He squeezed my shoulder, pulling me towards him and leaning his head against mine. "Thank you, Maggie." Silence again.

As we were pulling in my driveway, Peter said, "I've always thought you were quite the lady, Maggie. I even suspected that living alone and having so much responsibility might have given you a quirk or two." Even in the darkness I knew he was smiling.

"You're one in a million, Peter, quite a treasure, I think."

....

Two days later, I was having my second coffee outside when Peter drove in. He was smiling as he got out of his car and came over and sat down. "I've been worried, Maggie. I know you were stressed about the other night and I just wanted to make sure you're okay. It really is alright. I'm just glad you weren't trying to tell me something. Maybe next time, though, you could tell a fellow beforehand that you have something important to say, but that it's not personal."

"I'm sorry Peter. I really am. That wasn't the right time to say those things. I guess I didn't need to say them at all because they don't apply to you but maybe it helps you to understand me better.

"It's no secret that Amos and I had difficulties because of his illness, which meant I had to work more, and that meant more stress, and…and…did I just say more stress? I rolled my eyes. Stress was served up almost on a daily basis. To his credit, though, I didn't have to wait on him. If I was working and he wasn't, he usually had supper ready. There was one period when I was going through a depression and I'd come home and lie on the sofa while he made supper. Sometimes he helped me with my work - that was when I had the cleaning business - but he still made supper for us and let me rest.

"He often cooked for himself. And when he was

RHONDA CRONKHITE

working and I wasn't, he got up and got ready for work and made his own lunch. And he often did the dishes. In fact, he loved puttering in the kitchen, cleaning up. He did a better job than I do. And when I had company, he was wonderful. He'd cook things for us, often homemade French fries, and do the cleaning up while I enjoyed my company.

"Mentally, though, I carried a heavy load. It was mostly his inability to see things clearly without having it explained and then to be able to apply those guidelines to another situation if it wasn't the exact same circumstances. It was very stressful, to say the least.

"Except for the last few years when we were living apart, I carried more than my share of the load. I know I don't have that in me anymore. I'm sure I can carry my half, but I could never be in another relationship where I was responsible for more than half. It's just the way it is.

"The other thing, I'm old enough to realize that...well, Rachel, Sam's sister, says it best. She says that love changes. You couldn't live the rest of your life in the infatuated state you're in when you're first married. You'd never get anything done." I glanced away and when I looked back, I struggled to keep my face blank and said, "except maybe dishes." He just shook his head. "But love has a way of settling down and you become so comfortable with one another, more mature in your love. Then you don't even need to say a lot of things, you can read each other like a book.

"You might be so tired you want to drop, company has just left after you've worked all day, and the dishes are still left to do. I would see that and tell you to go sit in your chair and I'd get you a drink. I'll sit on your knee, then I will, I teased "and tell you how wonderful you are, how much I love you. I'll get you a soft blanket to cover up with."

"Can't wait," he said, eyes sparkling with anticipation.

"So those were the issues Amos and I had, besides his trouble in dealing with Luke.

"Then there's my mother - she had Dad so spoiled that she even combed his hair and brushed his teeth - the false ones. I'm sure she wished many times that she'd started out differently.

"I do believe in a man being the head of the home, but a head isn't a dictator. I think if more men knew what being the head meant, there'd be a lot more happy marriages. When it's done right, the head becomes almost invisible, it's just doing what it's meant to do - looking after things, taking care of things, being the strong one. It's not just men, either. Some women are overbearing, too, holding a whip.

"In all fairness, I'm probably a little too independent. Living alone forced me to find my inner strength. I realize that everyone does things differently and it's always easy to say, 'I couldn't deal with that' or 'I wouldn't put up with that' when you really don't know until you're there. But that's why I have such strong feelings."

"I'm glad you told me," he said.

RHONDA CRONKHITE

"I wish I'd done it differently, but it's done now and I'm glad you're okay. We don't need to talk about it anymore. We can move on." And that was that. I'd think the next time before I blurted something out.

"We had started to talk about how we'll share things. I certainly don't mind helping inside. Helping would be much better than doing it all," he said, biting his lip and looking like he wasn't really sure it was safe ground.

"That's good, because you'll be getting some help outside, too. I'm not giving all that up. That's my therapy."

"I have to put my dirty clothes in the hamper now," he said, "so I don't see any reason to change that. I can throw a load in the washer, too. I do it now. You might want to show me how you like things sorted, though. I'm probably not nearly as fussy as a woman would be. I will certainly continue to put my dishes in the sink. I might even help a certain lady with the washing if it's as exciting as she leads me to believe," he said, a mischievous twinkle in his voice.

"Peter, you stop teasing, now. I just said I might like helping a certain handsome fellow if he was doing dishes. If you heard anything else, you were reading between lines, and that can be dangerous."

"Okay. Okay. Right now I usually work three days a week. I leave around eight o'clock in the morning and am back by four-thirty or five o'clock. That's if I don't stop anywhere on the way," he said, grinning.

"Oh Peter! You'd best not be stopping anywhere."

He ignored my teasing. "You won't need to get up on the mornings I'm working but I wouldn't mind bringing you a cup of coffee, if you're awake."

"That would be nice, Peter, and any day you're trucking, I'll be happy to make supper. I think a man, or a woman, if that's the way it is, should have supper prepared for them when they get home from work. I might like making supper most of the time, but I certainly wouldn't mind having it made for me once in a while."

So what if the days I don't work, I get supper. We won't count Saturday and Sunday, so that leaves two days that I'll be home. Sundays we'll be going to church, so we'll probably just grab something quick, and we'll likely continue to go out for dinner with the kids, unless you'd rather not."

"Oh, I'd like that, unless we decide to invite someone for dinner occasionally. I enjoy having company. I don't usually eat breakfast early so maybe on Saturdays, we could just have brunch or an afternoon meal. If the kids still want to come Sunday evenings, I'd love that, too."

"You are a doll, Maggie. That would be nice."

"The nights you get supper, do you want me to do the dishes?" I asked. "Or would you like to do them together? You never know, there might be some writing between those lines," I said, giggling.

He shook his head, but couldn't hide the grin. "How about if we do the dishes together? I'll be looking after the big things outside – the mowing and plowing. Would the cleaning inside be a fair trade for that?"

"I'm sure it would be," I said, "but I don't clean every week like I used to. I just try to stay on top of things. If you're going to help with the laundry, I'll do the ironing."

"Well, I don't think we have any problems," he said. "It sounds all good to me. I just can't wait until we can put the plan into practice, can you?" He reached over, taking my hand in his. I nodded. "Mmm…yeah, it does sound rather exciting, doesn't it?"

Now we'd have to decide where we'd live. Would I be comfortable living at his place? Could we stay at his place part-time and mine part-time? The work would need to be kept up at both places.

Kendra had an idea she broached with her dad.

"We've been wondering, Dad, both Arnie and I, where you and Maggie plan to live. We wondered if you, or Maggie, will feel comfortable here. If you don't, Arnie and I would be glad to change houses with you until you decide. I'd love to be back home and it would give you time to make up your minds."

"That is so considerate of you two, Kendra. I'd have never expected an offer like that. For right now, we're going to sleep in the green room and Maggie will bring some of her things here to make it her place, too.

I'm not quite ready to let it go, and she feels the same about her place. We plan to try that for a year. If we do decide to sell, I'd love for you to have the house and I'd still be able to come here. That's a handsome thought, honey. You don't know what that means to me, for you to think of that. I'll certainly let Maggie know and we'll keep that in mind."

"We're so thrilled for you Dad, all of us. And the kids think she's pretty special." She giggled. "That Ben sure gave her a rough time at first didn't he? He let her know she wasn't walking into *his* life and taking on any special status without earning it."

Peter laughed. "He probably was just bold enough to say what the others were thinking. Except Marissa – she seemed to fall in love with Maggie just about as quick as I did." He paused, smiling. "I think in the end, Ben might have earned a little special status. Maggie seems to be quite taken with the little scallywag."

"She does, and it makes Ben feel quite important," Kendra said.

"You be sure and tell Arnie how much I appreciate your offer," Peter said.

"Why don't you come over for supper tonight, and you can tell him yourself."

Chapter 21

Warm Wishes

WE WERE STROLLING THROUGH THE GARDENS when Sherry and Brian arrived with my dad, Walter. Before long, my brother, Timothy, and his wife, Courtney, showed up. It seemed strange for them to come at the same time, unannounced. We were even more surprised when my sister Olivia, and her husband, Joe, along with their friends, Angie and John, arrived.

Before long, some of the neighbours started coming and we knew something was up. Tommy Woods became the spokesman. "We heard that you were planning a garden party, Maggie, so we decided to help you out. We also heard that you wanted everyone to bring a rock and you'd have prizes, so we just went ahead and brought our rocks. You can choose the ones for the prizes, but we brought the prizes, too."

My eyes widened in surprise as my hand flew to my chest, my mouth falling open. I couldn't breathe.

"You see," he went on, "we also heard that you have a wedding to plan. We're so delighted for you that we wanted to throw a party, so why not a garden party. Otherwise, you might get so excited about the wedding that you'd forget about the garden party. Since we've never had one around here, we didn't want to miss out on that, so we're all here to celebrate with you."

My mouth felt dry. "I...I...don't know what...to say," I stammered. "I'm so touched by your kindness. It's so nice of you all. Perhaps you'd like to take the lead, Tommy, and just let me know what you want me to do."

Just then, Luke and Kate drove in with the boys. Before long, Sebastian and Holly came, and before we knew it, Peter's children were there too. I was so overcome with emotion that I had to take a walk. My life had taken on a whole new dimension these last few months and I could barely contain my joy.

Luke found me in the picnic room. "You okay, Mom?" he asked.

Looking up at him, my eyes flooded with tears, overflowing into streams that I hoped didn't turn into rivers. I took his hand, not trusting my voice. Luke and I had truly been through a lot together. So many times I'd wished I could make everything right for him. But what is right, anyway? Isn't it all perspective?

I remembered looking out the kitchen window one day and seeing someone helping him out of his car. It was one of those moments when reality hit home. That was my son who couldn't get in or out of his car and had to depend on someone else for so many things. I know all the right answers, and most of the time, I'm okay, but sometimes a big rock comes galloping up my throat. I'd had a little pity party for a moment, and then wiped my eyes, set my shoulders, and got on with life. The reality is that he can do so many things. We both know we have a lot to be thankful for.

"I'll be okay," I managed to get out. "I think I'm just overwhelmed with all this happiness," I said, shaking my head, as I got up to get a napkin to wipe my eyes.

"It's about time, don't you think?" he said, and I noticed the tears glistening in his eyes.

I nodded. "I am happy, that's for sure," I said, going to the little sink he'd given me and splashing some cold water on my face. "I guess we'd better get back."

We were just rounding the corner of the house when we met Peter. He was looking for me. Noticing my red eyes, he asked, "You okay, Maggie? What's wrong?"

"You, I guess, Peter. Just you."

Astonished, he asked, "What did I do now?"

Taking his hand, I swung our arms backward and forward. "I just don't know what to do with all the happiness you create, darling." He gave me one of his special looks – the one that says 'there's not another like you, but I wouldn't change you for any other.'

The crowd was wandering around on the garden paths, admiring the fruits of some of my dreams. Some of the younger folks were roasting wieners and marshmallows at the fire pit and sitting on the three benches Amos and I had picked up from someone's trash.

Everyone liked the big rock, about four feet long, that we use as a bench. I'd placed it under a wild cherry tree, at an angle to the driveway. The rock is special because Luke and Amos had found it when they were doing some excavating and I'd wanted it so bad they'd kept working at it with a chain until they had it out of the hole. If there is a theme to my gardens, it would definitely be the rocks.

I got some ribbing about my grape vine. It was growing on ladders I had placed at an angle. I had planted it in a spot where there was nothing for support so that was the best I could find. And I don't like things straight. Straight to me sounds plain. You could say I don't just colour outside the lines, but I've been known to even move the lines. Maybe even remove them. The grapes would soon be ready for picking and making grape juice.

It was time to see whose rocks would be chosen as winners. Carl Brown won an arched trellis, the prize for the largest rock - shaped like a bicycle seat. Andrew Sewell won an Adirondack chair, well a knock-off of one, I should say, for the most unique rock, one that looked like a bear.

We were delighted with the beautiful wrought iron arbour they presented us with. I could already see roses growing up and around it, with my little wrought iron table and chairs setting near it.

After the last car had driven away, Peter suggested we take a stroll under the starlit sky. I listened to the chatter of the frogs wafting up from the brook. They say that some frogs are saying 'ribbit ribbit' but it sounded to me like 'love it love it.' Life was beautiful, felt even perfect. Although we both knew that couldn't be counted on for tomorrow, it sure did feel good right then.

When we went inside, Peter sat on the sofa while I got us a drink. When I passed him the glass, he set it on the end table and took my hand. "Sit with me, Maggie, just for a bit," he said, gently pulling me onto his lap. "It's okay, really."

I sat very still for a moment, my heart fluttering. I looked at him anxiously, then put my forehead against his and exhaled slowly.

"Are you okay?" he asked.

I nodded my head against his. "Yeah, I'll be alright." I swallowed, hearing the sound in my ears.

"I'm sorry, Maggie. I don't mean to make you uncomfortable, but I do like you sitting on my knee," he said, his usual mischievous grin in place.

"I like being here, too, but it is kinda close quarters, you know."

"Yeah, that's kinda what I had in mind," he said, biting his lip to keep from smiling.

After a few moments, I stood up. "I think I need a cup of coffee, Peter. Would you like one, too?"

"Yeah, that sounds like a good idea. But tell me, Maggie, you do trust me, don't you?"

I hesitated, biting my lip and knitting my brows together. "Oh, yes, Peter, I trust you. It's just," *How can I tell him I am just so conscious that Amos and I sat on this couch?* "We did say we'd be honest with each other, didn't we?" I asked.

"Yes, that's our agreement."

Throw it to the wind. Yes, just throw it to the wind. "I..., well, I don't know why I'm such a crack pot." I rubbed my hands together. *I have to get this out.* "I...I just keep seeing Amos and I sitting on this couch, and I know it's okay. Goodness me, I'm fifty-eight years old. At your place the other night, I kept thinking about you and Sandi snuggling up in your chair. I know that sounds stupid. We can't undo the past. I'm sorry, Peter." *There, it was out.*

"You do keep surprising me, Maggie. I thought you could take on the world," he said, chuckling. "I was wondering for a minute if maybe you didn't trust me." More seriously, he said, "It's okay, though, we'll be fine."

He studied me for a moment, then put his hand out and said softly, "Come here, Maggie." This time, I sat down on his knee and put my arm around his neck, pretending nothing had just happened.

"You've never given me any reason to not trust you, Peter. You've always been a perfect gentleman. I must say, though, that you could be pretty tempting. Your character is a big part of that. Well, no, everything about you is lovable. You're gorgeous to look at and you're beautiful inside. I feel like a pretty lucky lady."

He put his arms around me, holding me tight. "I love you Maggie, and I think I'm the lucky one. As long as we both feel that way, we'll always be happy. You can think that you got the best deal, but I'll know that I did. So there...you have it your way, and I'll have it mine."

"It's a deal," I said, getting up to get the coffee. We sat side by side on the sofa, me with one leg curled underneath myself as we sipped away, each lost in our own thoughts.

The last few months had gone by so quickly and so much had happened. It wasn't a long courtship but we both felt sure of our love and commitment to each other. We didn't see any need to wait. For what?

When he hugged me goodnight at the door, I wanted to stay in his arms forever.

"I do love you, Peter," I said, as he released me and took my hand.

"I know. And in a couple of weeks, I won't let you get away either."

"You'll have to catch me first," I teased.

Raising his eyebrow with a certain gleam in his eye, he said, "I think I've already caught you, Maggie LaHaye." I grabbed him roughly, laying my head against his chest.

When he said he really must be going, I begged him not to rush away. "I hate it when you leave," I said, loneliness already creeping into the air.

"I know, Maggie doll, I know. It's only two more weeks, though, and I'll never have to leave you again. It'll go by quickly."

"I don't believe you that it'll go by quickly, but I

suppose it will inevitably go by. I'm sorry, Peter, I'm such a baby."

"It's okay," he said, and kissed my forehead. "Goodnight, my love. I'll see you tomorrow."

"Goodnight darling." After just a moment, I couldn't resist saying "I'm so glad you caught me, Peter." The soft look in his eyes made me feel like a million dollars.

Chapter 22

I Do

OPENING MY EYES TO THE SUN STREAMING in the window, I jumped out of bed. Had I overslept? I checked the alarm clock, thankful that it was only six o'clock. There was no way I was going back to sleep. After all, this was the big day, October 11, the day Peter Weatherburn and I would be married. Today, I would be his wife in every sense of the word. Tingling all over with excitement, I felt more like eighteen than fifty-eight. Sometimes I still couldn't quite believe this was happening to me.

....

The little church was decked out for the occasion with pink and green ribbon and silver bells decorating a light green arbour at the front where the wedding party would stand. Each pew was graced with lily of the valley, tied with ribbons in different shades of purple. A big bouquet of lilies, pinks, purples, and light greens with lots of lily of the valley filled the earthen vase on the desk where we would sign the register. Acorns were scattered around the vase.

The desk was an antique and one of my favourites.

I'd got it from Chanda, my grandsons' mother. She was one of the fifty guests waiting excitedly for the big moment, anxious to meet this family who had become such an important part of her boys' lives.

Luke and I paused in the doorway before entering the sanctuary. Travis Tritt was singing softly, "My One And Only You." I needed a minute to process it all. *Can this really be happening to me? Can it be real?*

Then I saw Peter standing at the altar waiting for me, and I knew it was real. The flutter in my heart when I saw him couldn't have been imaginary. He was picture perfect handsome in his dark grey suit, purple shirt and lime green herringbone tie, with his beautiful locks combed neatly back. Beside him stood Judah, dressed in a grey suit and mauve shirt. I noticed him give Peter a friendly slap on the shoulder and whisper something in his ear.

Across the aisle, Rose stood proudly, wearing a lovely dark pink suit and mauve blouse, the lime green brooch I had given her for the occasion pinned to her collar. She was clutching a small bouquet of tiny pink and purple lilies with a smattering of lime green and white baby's breath throughout. She seemed to tremble a bit, from excitement, I suppose, and I knew her radiant smile was because of *my* happiness. What a sister!

Marissa and Ben had already started their walk down the aisle. Marissa, the flower girl, was dressed in a lime green dress with pink lilies in her hair and was carrying a basket of lily petals. Ben, dressed like his grampa, was the cutest little ring bearer ever. At least I thought so. But then, he had stolen my heart right along with his grampa.

Marissa smiled prettily, tossing pink and green silk leaves as she went. She turned back to find Ben, who should have been at her side, but he was sauntering slowly behind her, turning his head from side to side as he squinted up at the guests, looking completely bewildered. "Get up here, Ben," she whispered loudly, obviously annoyed at her little brother's antics.

Ben hurried forward. "What are they crying for?" he asked aloud, disgust colouring his voice as a few sniffles were heard and some of the ladies brushed happy tears from their eyes.

"Shush, Ben. Shush," his sister warned.

"Well, don't they know they're not supposed to cry at weddings? Grampa's getting married. And Maggie likes him, she said so."

"Of course she likes him, silly. Now shut up," Marissa hissed, now quite disgusted herself, but not at the guests.

When it was our turn, mine and Luke's, I smoothed the flowing skirt of my lime green suit and put my hand to my curls and lilac-coloured hat, checking them one more time. Putting my shoulders back, I took a deep breath just as Courtney struck the first note to "Here Comes The Bride." Suddenly, the excited audience was on their feet, turning towards the back.

My heart quickened as an almost inaudible gasp

spread through the room. I felt a sudden rush of emotion, flushing slightly as all eyes were on me. I had told myself I wouldn't be nervous. This was, after all, my third time of exchanging wedding vows. Still, a swarm of butterflies was buzzing around in my stomach.

When my eyes found Peter's, his look of love and approval thrilled my heart. I remembered how cute he'd looked when he'd asked if he could come calling, the day he'd brought the lovely pink lilies, just like the ones I was carrying today. I remembered those same butterflies, too, but today they were much more excited. After all, I would soon be the bride to that dashing man who had swept me off my feet, never to touch ground again, I suspected. *How I love him!*

Looking at Luke, his eyes were moist as I put my hand on his shoulder. "I love you, Mom," he whispered softly.

"I love you, too, darling."

I looked forward and my eyes met Peter's. The love I saw thrilled my heart, getting its rhythm all out of whack as I smiled endearingly at my soon-to-be husband. Peter's eyes, full of passion, were saying, *Come to me my love and let me take care of you for the rest of our lives, however long that may be.* My heart answered, *Yes, darling, I'll be right there. I can't wait!* I couldn't take my eyes off him as we made our way to the front, my knees and hands trembling with anticipation and excitement as we moved closer to the beginning of my wondrous new life and the man I loved with all my heart.

RHONDA CRONKHITE

The Unexpected Love

At last, we stood in front of Peter. The adoration I saw in his eyes near did me in. It was all I could do to keep from throwing myself into his arms, but I would do this right.

Peter's eyes spoke volumes as he looked at Luke. "Thank you, Luke," he said. Luke smiled and nodded, as Peter took my hand, surprising me by lifting me off my feet and twirling me around to his left side, setting me down in my place. The wedding party was beaming.

The guests were ecstatic at this spontaneous act. It sounded like my nephew, Tim, who cheered, "Maggie and Peter, Woo Hoo." Then several others chimed in, "Woo Hoo, Woo Hoo." There didn't appear to be a dry eye in the place, including mine. Turning to look at Peter, I saw that he was blinking back tears, too. Grinning from ear to ear, Ben announced in a rather loud whisper, "That's my new gramma!" Soft chuckles rippled through the audience.

We continued facing our friends and families, the minister standing with his back to them. It doesn't make sense to me having the minister facing the people. He wasn't the one getting married nor was it him everyone had come to see today.

Pastor Jack took a moment to recover from these unrehearsed events. "Well, friends, that about says it for how happy we are for Maggie and Peter. It's such a pleasure to be here today, to be a part of this happy occasion. Now, let me just find my place so we can move on," he said, seeming flustered as he scanned his program.

"Oh!" he said, looking up. "With all the excitement, I almost forgot. I think we have yet another surprise. Your children," he continued, looking to the bride and groom, "tell me that you gave them quite a serenade the other night, and they think it would be nice to hear it again. They say Peter was a little jealous over Maggie's dogs, so I can't even imagine what we're in for."

Closing my eyes, I let my breath out slowly. *I'm not sure if I can do this.* Peter smiled, in spite of the warm pink creeping from his collar. "What do you say? You started it."

Looking at Dad, sitting in the front row, I said, "This is really your fault, Dad, for teaching me to be so silly."

"Peter, let's do the first lines together. That will make it easier." He nodded, taking my hands as I turned to face him. Courtney, being part of the scheme, started playing softly.

Smiling at Peter, I gathered all my courage, as we began. I decided to pretend there was no one there but Peter and me. Looking up at him, I was sure my eyes were shining with the love I felt. I put all my heart into every word I was singing to this wonderful man who had made my life worth living again, who loved me, quirks and all.

When Peter sang his words, a tear rolled, unbidden, down my cheek as he proudly declared that he couldn't stand not having his Maggie around, so had decided he'd best keep me. His loving smile told me he would do it in a heartbeat, wouldn't even think twice. Only I knew the depth of what he was proclaiming.

Another thunderous applause erupted as we finished.

Joining our right hands, I said my vows to Peter, looking into his eyes as I promised him that I would love, honour and obey...'til death us do part.

Taking both my hands, Peter surprised me with vows of his own. With eyes mirroring the affection so clear in his voice, he began, "I, Peter Weatherburn, do take thee, Maggie LaHaye, to be my cherished wife. To love you forever with all that I am, to live each day in a way that will make your life richer and sweeter." Almost as an afterthought, he grinned, "so that you really will believe you're the happiest woman alive."

With unabashed devotion, he continued, "You've changed my life, Maggie. I can't even imagine my life without you in it. You've taught me how to laugh and have fun again. You may have even turned back the clock when I wasn't looking because I don't feel as old as I did before I hauled that first load of soil for you." I feared I might not be able to hold the tears back.

"I promise to do my best to be the man you deserve, to love and care for you forever." With his face glowing, he continued softly, "I love you, Sweetheart. Will you have me...Maggie LaHaye?"

I couldn't stop myself. "Oh, Peter," cried, throwing my arms around his neck. Through a torrent of tears, I sobbed, "Have you? You've had my heart for a long,

long time." Choking back the sobs, I laughed, "Maybe from the first day you hauled that soil. Of course, I'll have you. Forever," I said. "I love you so much, Peter Weatherburn. I love you so much."

Poor Ben. He must have been really miffed by now. There were so many sniffles, it sounded like the whole church was crying.

My sister, Sherry, sang "Thanks To The Keeper Of The Stars" just before the register was signed. That's another one of my oddities. Having someone sing while the register is signed reminds me of having a special sung in church while the offering is being taken. And besides, I wanted to be able to enjoy the song, too. So the wedding party stood quietly, listening to the beautiful words, beautiful to us anyway. We both knew what second chances were about and were thrilled at being given another chance.

As Peter and I signed, Courtney began playing "I Wouldn't Change You If I Could." When we finished, Jeff and Sheri Easter took over, via video, while the others signed. Taking advantage of the music, Peter whispered, "You look lovely, Mrs. Weatherburn."

I smiled sweetly. "You're pretty easy on the eyes yourself, Mr. Weatherburn."

Reaching in his pocket, he took out a small package. "I thought you might like this," he said quietly, handing me the box. Opening it, I gasped to see a white gold watch with stones matching my rings. I looked at him adoringly, but no words would come.

As Pastor Jack presented Mr. And Mrs. Peter Weatherburn to the audience, all formality (what little was left) was tossed to the wind as our family and friends clapped enthusiastically. "It's Such A Pretty World" with Wynn Stewart began playing as the wedding party marched out.

I was thrilled to be Mrs. Peter Weatherburn. Oh, I couldn't wait to get on with this new chapter of my life. Looking at Peter and laughing, I said, "Yes, Maggie Weatherburn does have a nice ring to it. I like it already."

He laughed, squeezing my hand tighter. "I thought you would."

Peter's car was waiting, trimmed with lime green and pink ribbons, with all kinds of cans and noisemakers tied on behind. We got in, waiting for Sebastian and Holly, who would drive us to the reception. Putting his arm around my shoulder, Peter asked softly, "Are you happy, Maggie?"

My heart was overflowing. "I'm very happy, Peter. And very contented."

"So am I. You're awfully good medicine, Maggie LaHaye, I mean Maggie Weatherburn," he said, grinning, as he squeezed me closer.

I laid my head on his shoulder for a moment. *Oh, I can't resist!* Turning to look at him, eyes sparkling with excitement and joy, barely able to control the smile that so wanted to burst into laughing, I said, "Are you glad you didn't leave me when you found out I was a little silly, Peter, darling?"

With his signature teasing grin, his response was instant. "I still haven't decided whether you're silly or not." I barely heard Sebastian and Holly getting in the car. "You do add a lot of colour with your love and laughter, my sweetest Maggie doll. I don't think I'd trade you for the black and white version. Not even if I could."

Sebastian was looking in the mirror. "Well said, Grampa Peter. Nor would I. Keep all the black and white nannies, I'll take my colourful one any day." He started the engine and there was Jeff and Sheri singing our song again, "I Wouldn't Change You If I Could."

"Oh, Peter," I said, turning and throwing my arms around him. "I never thought I could be so happy again. I feel like I'm walking on air...well, sitting on air," I laughed.

He squeezed me tight. "Our hearts are home, Maggie."

As he put his arm around my neck, I laid my head back on his shoulder and reached up, putting my hand over his. Although I was as happy as I'd ever been, a single tear found its way out the corner of my eye, rolling down my cheek. Peter noticed and wiped it away with his thumb.

There was no need for words.

The End

P.S. "I ALMOST FORGOT," I said, remembering the package I'd had Sebastian leave on the seat. Peter was speechless, too, when he opened it to find a white gold watch matching his wedding ring.

The stars were sure shining on us today. I hoped they'd always shine so brightly.

About The Author

Rhonda Cronkhite comes from a small rural community in New Brunswick, the picture province of Canada. Nestled amongst the vast evergreens and beautiful flowing waters of the Saint John River, it is a uniquely inspirational setting. Using real life events to shape and mold all her writing endeavours, her passion is to touch the heart and soul of those who can relate to the stories she tells.

And she likes to tell it as it is, at least as it is according to Rhonda. ☺ She doesn't do any sugar coating, either, whether she's delivering a touching eulogy or just giving you her honest-to-goodness opinion. You'll usually get a laugh or two, even at her expense. Writing has become a great source of comfort, introspection, and fun.

"The Unexpected Love" is her first book, available in Kindle format on Amazon and in paperback from

CreateSpace.

Rhonda would love to hear your feedback on what you thought of her book. If you enjoyed "The Unexpected Love," feel free to send your comments to unexpectedlove2017@gmail.com.

Another great way to share this inspiring love story and help spread the word about this new author is to "Like" her on Facebook. Her author page is Rhonda Cronkhite.

A Word From Rhonda's Heart

It's been a bittersweet journey telling this story. It's brought back not only memories tucked away, but the feelings and emotions I felt in that other life. It seems, in a way, like another life, and yet it's all so very much a part of me, a part of who I've become.

Although it was a huge loss, I don't feel cheated. Rather, I feel that I've been very blessed. The love that George and I shared was not an ordinary love, at least it seemed that way to me. It was more like a consuming love, which can be kinda scary when one has no experience with love.

A few times during the forty years since George has been gone, I've awoken from a dream where I realized immediately that it was just a dream, but the special love we shared was there in the room and I was reminded anew of what I'd lost.

Back in our courting days, we didn't see each other every day and talk on the phone a dozen times a day like they do today. Or maybe it's texting a dozen times a day, today. :) We saw each other every two or three weeks in the beginning and in the end, every week. We wrote letters, and more letters, between visits, and we always talked on the phone on weekends, if we didn't get together.

I'm not sure at what point I went from being badly in love, to being madly in love with George, but I suppose it must have been about the time that Paulette, almost three years younger than I, gave me a smarting lecture.

When George left, even though Paulette and I shared a bedroom, I went to the safety of my room, threw myself on my bed, and cried. I hated it! Paulette was disgusted. "Grow up!" she stormed, one day. But as in the story, when George came back, my world was right again.

I never wanted our hugs to end. As Maggie puts it, I wanted to stay in his arms forever. George, being a dreadful tease, as he was trying to pull away to go to work one day, chuckled and said, "I'll have to give you a baby so you'll have part of me here and you won't be lonely while I'm gone." I laughed. I didn't know that in a year's time, I'd be so glad to have that baby, a part of him that I could keep.

As the story between Maggie and Peter has unfolded, I've read it several times and I've rarely got through it without tears. It was a wonderful chapter of my life and I wouldn't trade a whole lifetime of everyday chapters for that one chapter. It was well worth the price. After all, to love is always to risk losing, and to experience that kind of love is priceless.

The story seems so real that I find myself thinking that perhaps Peter Weatherburn is lurking around the corner somewhere. I don't think there were many created from that mold, but it does make one wonder.

..

Disclaimer

While I'm aware that a good story should have some conflict to make it more interesting, after careful consideration, I've decided to go with my original idea, which is to present this story as it was.

While it's true that George and Rhonda should have had a few conversations that they didn't know how to approach, it's also true that they never had a fight. As you've seen, the mature Maggie knows how to broach whatever crosses that crazy mind of hers. So there would be no such unsaid stuff today.

Rhonda was obsessed with George and couldn't get enough of him. She resented his best friend, who lived next door, arriving at their home almost before George had finished his supper. And he stayed until bedtime. She loved Ken too, but enough was enough. She wishes she'd known how to tell George how she felt, or that he'd clued in to her feelings.

When George asked if they could invite her uncle and grandparents to dinner one day after church, she hunched her shoulders. She didn't know how to say that she was afraid she wouldn't be able to make a big dinner on her own. She'd done lots of cooking at home, but it was different to be totally responsible for the ordeal without her mom to make sure everything came out right. And George didn't know he could have offered to help her. He just knew he'd be proud to show off what he knew his wife could do.

So to invent conflict between George and Rhonda here for the sake of following the norm would mar the story, at least in my opinion. And I've never been one to follow the norm.

I've kept all characters true to who they are/were.

I've also gone against professional advice and decided to include a picture of George and Rhonda. If I were reading this story, I'd love to see the real people.

George and Rhonda

Rhonda does look like she has the world by the tail, or at least thinks she does.

Contact Rhonda

Visit www.TheUnexpectedLove.com to see what others are saying about the crazy Maggie and also to listen to the songs. It's hard to say what you might learn.

Drop me a note at unexpectedlove2017@gmail.com if you have comments. I'd love to hear from you!